THE LEGACY SERIES

What We Might Become
Sara Reish Desmond

The Silver State Stories
Michael Darcher

An Instinct for Movement
Michael Mattes

The Machine We Trust
Tim Conrad

Gridlock
Brett Biebel

Salt Folk
Ryan Habermeyer

The Commission of Inquiry
Patrick Nevins

Maximum Speed
Kevin Clouther

Reach Her in This Light
Jane Curtis

The Spirit in My Shoes
John Michael Cummings

*The Effects of Urban Renewal on Mid-Century America and
Other Crime Stories*
Jeff Esterholm

What Makes You Think You're Supposed to Feel Better
Jody Hobbs Hesler

Fugitive Daydreams
Leah McCormack

Hoist House: A Novella & Stories
Jenny Robertson

Finding the Bones: Stories & A Novella
Nikki Kallio

Self-Defense
Corey Mertes

Where Are Your People From?
James B. De Monte

Sometimes Creek
Steve Fox

The Plagues
Joe Baumann

The Clayfields
Elise Gregory

Kind of Blue
Christopher Chambers

Evangelina Everyday
Dawn Burns

Township
Jamie Lyn Smith

Responsible Adults
Patricia Ann McNair

Great Escapes from Detroit
Joseph O'Malley

Nothing to Lose
Kim Suhr

The Appointed Hour
Susanne Davis

"Set in the same former mill town and spanning many eras, David Ricchiute's collection of closely observed, elegantly wrought stories exposes secrets people keep from their community, their families, and themselves. From lies about embezzlement to generations of broken promises over Native lands, from hidden indignities of the polio epidemic to more modern scourges of mill-town-aftermath pollution, Ricchiute's insightful stories draw energy from the clash of truth and nostalgia while probing the corroding effects of carrying guilt and secrets."

—JODY HOBBS HESLER
author of *Without You Here*

"'Longing,' we're told in David Ricchiute's *Keeping What's Best Left Kept Secret*, engenders 'reckless behavior,' and, indeed, one of the many pleasures of reading this poignant and lyrical story collection is witnessing that force at work as the boys and sons and husbands and fathers and divorced and single men glimpsed in these pages seek (and often fail) to quell an unnamed but pervasive yearning. By turns mysterious, melancholic, and deeply moving, Ricchiute's book reaches into life's many and varied rooms—in hospitals and homes, schools and churches, hotels and libraries—to expose and penetrate humanity, in all its complexity, its marvels and regrets, miscommunications and betrayals. *Keeping What's Best Left Kept Secret* is a work of haunting beauty by an exciting and perceptive writer."

—LEAH MCCORMACK
author of *Fugitive Daydreams*

KEEPING WHAT'S BEST LEFT KEPT SECRET

stories

DAVID RICCHIUTE

CORNERSTONE PRESS
UNIVERSITY OF WISCONSIN-STEVENS POINT

Cornerstone Press, Stevens Point, Wisconsin 54481
Copyright © 2025 David Ricchiute
www.uwsp.edu/cornerstone

Printed in the United States of America by
Point Print and Design Studio, Stevens Point, Wisconsin

Library of Congress Control Number: 2024948513
ISBN: 978-1-960329-63-9

Cover art: "Sculpteur Devant sa Sellette, avec un Spectateur Barbu (Sculptor in front of his easel, with a bearded spectator)" by Pablo Picasso (1966) (private collection)

This is a work of fiction. Names, characters, businesses, places, events, and incidents are either the products of the author's imagination or used in a fictitious manner. Any resemblance to actual persons, living or dead, or actual events is purely coincidental.

Cornerstone Press titles are produced in courses and internships offered by the Department of English at the University of Wisconsin–Stevens Point.

DIRECTOR & PUBLISHER
Dr. Ross K. Tangedal

EXECUTIVE EDITORS
Jeff Snowbarger, Freesia McKee

EDITORIAL DIRECTOR
Ellie Atkinson

SENIOR EDITORS
Brett Hill, Grace Dahl

PRESS STAFF
Paige Biever, Madalyn Carpenter, Zoie Dinehart, Mai Kao Hang, Karlie Harpold, Lillian Kulbeck, Allison Lange, Christiana Niedzwiecki, Sophie McPherson, Hannah Rouer, Ava Willett

to Grace, Mia, Eva, Lea, Charlotte, & Louie
—treasures, every one of them

STORIES

I.

Indifferent Limbs 1
Nights 15
Beached on White Sheets 16
Isn't It Better That She Knows? 24
How Much I Must Have Looked Like Her to Her 26
Their Version 32
The Card Catalog 34
Two-Thirty 39
Angst 43
The Body Double of Making Do 48

II.

An Absence of Speech 61
Standing Perfectly Still on the Table 64
Done at Thirty 69
Carp 71
What Scrimshaw Leaves Unsaid 74
A Daughter's Conviction 77
Inside the Jewelry Store Window 79
Is This a Good Time? 82
You Sure This Here's the One? 103
Where This Was Going 107
How Could I Get Away With This? 111

III.

None but the Most Diminished Hopes 121

Acknowledgements 185

. . . pardon that thy secrets should be sung.
—John Keats, "Ode to Psyche"

I.

Indifferent Limbs

Near a creek where his mother said, *Don't dare go,* a young boy spots a garter snake, jaws surrounding a half-swallowed worm, compelling the boy to bend at the knees, starting the descent toward the lumbering snake. It's then that he buckles from weakness in his legs, ignored for days as a nuisance that passes—like a brain freeze, maybe, or a parent's stare—something like anything a child overlooks, until the nuisance firms its grip.

Alone, the stunned boy crawls to the road, elbows dragging dormant legs, belt buckle scraping gravel and grass that spills in under his underpants. *Don't,* she'd said, *don't dare go,* to a young man bent on freedom and adventure, reduced for now to a boy again, blocks away from the mother he defied—and miles away from a puzzled girl, sitting on the edge of her new twin bed. Much like children everywhere, she ignored the symptoms she barely felt. First in the form of a misplaced step in a sequence of others that landed in place. Then in weakness before the step that accelerated with no other warning, the steps arriving at the floor underfoot before the girl or the floor expects.

Put on your shoes, the mother says. *The new Mary Janes from Cherry & Webb.*

Mama! the girl cries to her mother. *Mama?*

The mother, oblivious to errant steps but certain the cries have a truth their own, finds the girl sprawled out on the floor—lifeless legs hopelessly immobile, a mind of their own, indifferent limbs.

All this happens, as it did for the boy, to a child whose health was taken for granted, like anyone takes good health for granted. She'd driven alone in a soapbox derby, delivered papers on a morning route, climbed the schoolyard's jungle gym—more, far more, than most children did. But most children weren't looking up from the floor, up to a mother whose face had fallen, hopeful she'd waxed the floor too often, awakened at once to what this was.

IN ANOTHER MONTH, THE LEAVES would have fallen, followed soon by seasonal frost, slowing, then ending, the frightful assault.

In a driveway, a father says, *God, why now?*

In a car, a mother says, *But for a month.*

On successive days, overcast days, the parents of the boy and the parents of the girl, otherwise unaware of the other, admit the terrified boy and girl, lungs unable to breathe on their own, to a dedicated ward on a leafy campus—"Chapin" for short, Chapin Clinic, the city's one hope for infectious disease. A placard in the lobby reads POLIO-MYELITIS and offers etymology from the Greek—"polio" for the gray shade of spinal cord matter, "myelitis" for inflamed marrow.

If you'd arrived at Chapin, a child in tow, you'd have struggled to summon the courage to read it, or to come to grips with leaving the child. You wouldn't know—you couldn't know—that *then*—that moment—you wouldn't remember, or the moment you frantically dialed numbers, or drove your child to the clinic in traffic, or confronted doctors absorbed in the moment as well as you'd remember the emptiness after—after you gathered the child's clothes, after a nurse took the child away, after the days and nights thereafter, waiting, waiting in deafening silence, seated with others but thoroughly alone, looking, staring, at door after door, each door closed, latched, imposing, each one a portal to another unknown.

The arrival of a long-evaded terror delivers a form of relief too, like giving-in when you know you've drowned.

PHOTOS WERE RELEASED OF POLIO WARDS, but Chapin staff thought the scene too grim. Row after row of iron lungs, 800 pounds and seven feet long, arranged in symmetrical, herringbone patterns, each with a child, strikingly inert, a lung's respirator mimicking lungs in wards with nurses in stark-white smocks attending to bodies reduced to faces, some with the pimples puberty brings, none with wrinkles or signs of age.

Placed no more than a few lungs apart, the boy and the girl notice little—other than a ceiling high above, a mirror placed at an angle before them, and the droning wheeze of mechanical lungs that sounds to the children like pure white noise. The girl tells her mother the noise is a comfort, *Knowing others are in one too,* she says as the mother gathers to leave, the father arranging his hat at the door.

In the lobby, the father and mother of the girl pause at an oddly affecting display. A box-sized replica of an iron lung, a collection box the clinic placed for the National Foundation of Infantile Paralysis—called more commonly the "March of Dimes," first by the singer Eddie Cantor and then by everyone else—founded by Franklin Delano Roosevelt, at age thirty-nine, a victim himself.

The boy's parents, walking slowly, don't see the girl's parents in the hall, standing no more than a few feet away.

If only God would let them limp, the boy's mother says to the father.

I'd settle for that, the father says, leaving the boy in the *polio ward*, he learns to say, reluctantly say, when someone asks how the boy is doing.

In the ward, from the ceiling, mobiles hang where neither the boy nor the girl can see, engaged entirely in what they remember. School yard slides, popsicle sticks, bicycles, lollipops, favored toys—none of which were designed to remember in the way that things in the ward remember. *Remember* is what a respirator does, belts wheezing to animate breath. *Remember* is what a tank does, sealing the pressure that enables breath. *Remember* is what a mirror does, recording remnants of a child's breath. The respirator, tank, and mirror know that the mind forgets what the body forgot. Body and mind need the other to happen. Neither of the two, as if they are two, ever quite works alone.

IN THE 1950S, POLIO SPREAD—beginning in summer, ending in fall—arriving each year to the nation's inbox through television, newspapers, and magazines. TV and print upped the ante on a lurking, seasonal epidemic. Throughout the nation thousands were afflicted, among them the adolescent girl and boy, settled now in a polio ward, each repeatedly asking about a younger brother at home. Knowing the nation, the world, was watching, President Eisenhower, decorated in war, diverted the nation's coast-to-coast angst into a call for hope. He interviewed virologists, absorbed their work, and embraced a guarded public resolve that science would come to bear, albeit in the face of a private apprehension that science may well fail.

Trials on 1.8 million children confirmed to statistically significant levels that Jonas Salk's new antibody, compiled from dead polio cells—administered to Salk's own family, no less—was safe and effective in double-blind trials that delivered vaccine to half the children and saline solution to an unwitting half who suffered more often the signs of disease than children in the vaccine sample did. Meeting in the White House with Jonas Salk, Eisenhower, overcome with emotion, broke down before him in tears.

The parents of the girl and the parents of the boy cheered the altogether promising news, aware there'd be no cure for the stricken, but hopeful the vaccine would spare the gait of each of their younger children. *Mixed feelings,* the girl's mother said. *Too late?* the boy's father said to himself.

Months later, everything changed.

Dramatizing the urgency of reaching the masses, five pharmaceutical houses, subjected to a rigorous competition, secured a vaccine-production license, all on a single day. But in a twist-of-fate of heartbreaking proportions, one of the licensed pharmaceuticals failed to eradicate live polio cells in two supervised production pools, producing vaccine with a lethal virus given unknowingly to healthy children, most in the first and second grades. The virus paralyzed fifty, killed five, incited an epidemic in the families stricken, and presented parents throughout the country—including the parents of the girl and the boy, each mindful of a healthy child at home—with a choice that tormented many of them. Inoculation of healthy children would require a parent's informed consent, a risky choice when the state of knowledge was modest at best. Together at home at night alone, the boy's parents prayed, the girl's parents probed, and came by their panic honestly.

In spite of trials gone tragically awry, parents arrived at a guarded calm, aware of the risks inoculation brings but floundering blindly in feeble precautions—avoid swimming pools, creeks, and groups; suppress the urge to mingle in crowds—while awaiting a protocol the government sanctioned. In this case, announced by the President himself on a Tuesday two months into spring, *States will advise … as*

*to their general plans for distribution of the vaccine ... Every
parent and child should be grateful.*

And the parents of the girl and the boy *were* grateful—to
him and to scientists the President named. But not to the
National Academy Committee which, hoping to target
the most vulnerable ages, recommended a priority the
President adopted and announced to an anxious nation.
First to children ages five to nine.

The girl's mother says, *No, no!*

The boy's father says, *Priority to who?*

The mother's younger son was four. The father's younger
son was three.

EYES FOCUSED INSIDE OF THEMSELVES, the boy is unable
to see the hair his fingers find below his waist and the girl
is unable to see the breasts her fingers feel below her neck.

Neither is able, hands by their side, to punctuate their
voice and speech with gesturing fingers or waving hands,
the impenetrable wall of the iron lung having reduced their
arms to silence. And what of the longings to come thereafter,
adolescents assembled in rows of lungs, others beside them
left and right—and the sets of parents who think of this,
torn between sleep and consciousness?

And what to make of watchful neighbors, some overcome
with divisive caution, among them a couple who knew the
boy? Together at a window, curtains drawn, the couple, coaxing a toddler to sleep, look—then stare—across the way to
the clapboard house where the parents of the boy, housed at
Chapin, open their door and walk to the street hand-in-hand
with their younger son, dressed as a clown for Halloween.
The couple dims the first floor lights, sits in the dark in an
upstairs hall, and stays there till the evening's over, ignoring
knocks at their front door.

And what of the things that were left behind? On different
days, into the night, the mother of the girl, the father of the

boy, reaches, reaches—under a bed, into a drawer—to find a now abandoned shoe, her a dark blue Mary Jane; him an off-white, high top Converse that the mother and the father hold in their hands longer than they had a reason to. And what to think of the boy's grandmother, no longer able to live alone, probing closely a whisker on her chin, breath lingering on a mirror longer than the patience the grandmother had for prayer. She turns from the mirror to the boy's mother, a book on her lap, a glass in her hand. *Take what's given,* she says to the mother, who says to the father, *A sip of this?* The mother passes the glass to the father, whose gaze toward the mirror is steely, cold.

WERE IT NOT FOR THE WHEEZE of iron lungs, you could hear the steps of faithful nurses delivering care at Chapin Clinic, some of the care progressive for the time. They applied hot packs on tender spasms, exercised atrophied legs and arms, massaged the children's backs and bottoms where sores or blisters were prone to form.

Younger nurses were on at night, save for one—called Sister Mary, though she wasn't a nun—who patiently listened and attentively watched, up on her toes, searching, walking, then suddenly moving to a waiting child, who knew that when the occasion called, she'd smile warmly, reach in her pocket, and dab a tissue around their eyes, among them the girl, among them the boy, who relied on Sister several nights, until they learned to hold it in, turning instead to what was near.

From her pillow, the girl could see the windows, opened slightly from the afternoon, repelling rain that sounds to the girl like the comforting chorus that fell at night on the roof of the carport below her room. From his pillow, the boy could see the wall that supports a row of radiator pipes spitting a series of hissing clicks that sound to the boy like knuckles cracking, just like he often heard from his own. From their pillows, the girl and the boy could see what few who entered could bear to see—a collection of rows of dependent children, bodies entombed in iron lungs, weeks or months from readjustment or from a turn to a fate untold. Later, each of them noticed more. All of the children noticed more.

The ceiling, a clock, overhead lights, windows, radiators, horizontal blinds, tables, blankets, surgical gloves, pitchers of water, a checkerboard floor. A sink, faucets, plumbing pipes, electrical outlets, plugs in the wall, an open box of glass syringes positioned on an upright cabinet shelf. Swabs, bottles, an empty basket, beds the kids called "cookie trays" that slid in and out of the iron lungs, portal windows seamlessly mounted on the sides of seven-foot iron lungs, smaller portals on the "little kid" lungs. A spoon, a carafe, paper cups, a tissue box, candy, leather gloves, a gurney the girl hadn't seen before, a pair of automatic swinging doors that leads where some of the children go.

To the parents of a child who's seen these things, a dogged obsession demands in spades that the first steps taken to treat the child be taken to bring a cure. Most hope the stricken will find their way—*from* iron lung *to* wheelchair and brace; *from* innocent youth *to* middle age—with little more than a memory in tow. Few think at first there'll be no cure and fewer think the worst.

Less than a month in Chapin Clinic, the parents of the boy sit by the boy and watch him slip into death. An open casket, reprieve from the lung, allowed the parents to see him again, whole from head to toe. Fourteen hundred died that year, but he was the one his parents buried with a calm that friends who knew them well attributed to faith.

ON A COLD, COLD, HOWLING-COLD NIGHT—not, for some reason, a pleasant night—the boy's grandmother, half a mind left, limping in only a frayed half-slip, opened the door and stepped outside, *To call him,* she said to the boy's mother.

Looking at her mother—confused, silent—how could she hope for more for her mother, or more for herself, or for anyone who thinks the ways of a mother otherwise end with the mother? Unless there's a way to pick up and go. If not in a way her conscience forbid, then maybe just once in momentary flight—shedding in flight the devastating grief but with spirit, commitment, confidence, and spunk, allowing for once, if never again, the lifting of body, of courage and guile, in a free pirouette from anguish and fear, all in the midst of a family in need—a faithful husband, a son at home—bringing to the knees all who would witness much less a scene few could imagine than silence now that the boy is gone.

TO SURVIVORS WHO ENDURED POLIO'S WRATH, neither dormant legs nor an iron lung foretold the threat that abuse would become. One-third of eleven hundred polio survivors revealed in a decades-later study more contemporaneous physical abuse than an equivalent number of non-disabled—like arduous exertion to inflame pain, beatings to motivate movement or breath.

Nine-in-ten polio survivors revealed more emotional abuse than an equivalent number of non-disabled—like bystanders ridiculing "human freaks," classmates berating "cripples." And three-in-ten helpless children endured unthinkable abuse, described in vignette by the study's author. *If there was a pedophile in the family or on a hospital staff …you can guess what might have happened.*

What could explain studies reporting the stoic resolve of polio victims—calm, poised, uncommonly erect—concealing their disability and keeping their secrets all to themselves?

And how would raindrops falling on a roof sound years later to the girl?

ERADICATION DISARMS PRECAUTION for no reason other than memory fades with each passing year and generation. But as time goes by, virologists know, viruses mutate in hideous forms, divining schemes to present in hosts before immunity or inoculation can hold the mutant's havoc at bay.

Her mother and father long deceased, their memories of torment only their own, the girl, now aging, her brother gone, is alarmed to read that hundreds of children in a single year—and equivalent numbers in biannual years—had fallen victim to paralytic conditions that began with symptoms disturbingly different from decades before. A boy's face droops, an eyelid drops, and his throat is unable to swallow whole. A girl's eyes move independently, and her speech is slurred and slow.

Able to walk since her early teens—a full recovery, experienced by many for reasons or remedies no one knows—she worries that her daughter's only daughter, the age now that she was then, may be at risk for what science calls acute flaccid myelitis—or AFM, as the doctors say—a condition reported in a number of states, one the state her granddaughter's in.

She calls her daughter some distance away to ask if maybe she's heard or knows, thinking her daughter had to know or, if she didn't, would want to know.

No, I haven't. I'll call later, she says to her stunned and deflated mother with none of the overt preoccupation parents in the '50s came to display.

Damn, the mother says out loud after her daughter hangs up the phone.

Not polio, no, but a spinal disease that presents in ways that polio didn't. Even before the arrival of symptoms, it begins in seemingly harmless ways—nasal congestion, diarrhea, a runny nose, a sinus infection—then accelerates with dramatic force from one or more antecedents to indiscriminate full on attacks on neural tissues in the spinal cord that seize the body, legs, or face, presenting symptoms like polio—though samples are free of polio, leaving the Centers for Disease Control with a contradictory pair of options, a virus or an autoimmune condition?

Then what to do if either's the one or, if not, neither or both—or, if not, then something else virologists think could be at play: environmental toxins, genetic disorders, or a hundred or so enteroviruses, one that surfaced in symptomatic children but not in enough to offer a lead. Given no cure or means for prevention, victims have little recourse but hope that rather than lead to a breathing aide, symptoms turn mild, forgiving, and brief.

Appearing in numbers unexpectedly, AFM is a rare but debilitating condition of unknown source or probable cause, though increasingly clear to family doctors presented with symptoms in helpless children and news reports across the nation on TV, online, and in print. Lacking the immunities adults have built, infants and children are most at risk, both for symptoms and for diagnosis, since biopsy in the most definitive form requires a sample from nerves in the spine, cautioning doctors to rely instead on a less revealing but safer sample—a stricken child's spinal fluid.

Wash your hands, … Cover your face, offer little in the way of comfort, just as they didn't decades before. *Only one chance in a million,* they say—despite spikes in alternating years, evidence of a patterned biannual normal—suggesting occurrence is relatively rare. But "only" was little consolation in an article the mother saw by chance. *Collapsed mid-stride,* a mother had said, *like a hapless chorus of marionettes.* One day intact, the next immobile.

Not unlike the 1950s, a mystery of causes delivers its effects in a child paralysis that struck with irony the healthy son of a Weill Institute child neurologist, stumped by the company the causes keep, aware how meager small comforts feel, and aware how little there is to tell—but committed deeply to lend communion to parents alone at a child's side, witnessing a dwindling range of motion the body declines to volunteer and awaiting the onset of limb-length discrepancy, motor impairment, and a medical literature on rehabilitation for children parents nurtured in health but hadn't begun to dream for.

Days later, her distant daughter still hasn't called. "A polio victim," she writes in a draft of a handwritten note she contemplates sending her baffling daughter. "You don't feel what we all felt?" she asks in darker, bolder ink, then adds two exclamation points. She jots down words like "reckless, careless, thoughtless, cruel" then thinks better of sending the note.

IN HER BEDROOM, ALONE, SETTING her hair, she stews that her daughter hasn't called. And after she said, *I'll call,* like daughters and sons have said since the '50s, when phones first offered a chance to hedge.

Seated at a desk, the daughter searches—screen after screen—on words she thinks her mother said, then settles at a site reporting news from a major Midwest paper. She learns her mother's alarm has merit and reads that a Washington University surgeon harvests nerves in a child's toes to then reroute to the child's legs, allowing some children the hope and potential to someday stand or walk again.

Still, she hasn't called her mother. Instead, she exploits her mother's lead and sits by a window thoroughly impressed that much like Salk did decades before, the surgeon, roughly her own age, restores the lives of impaired children.

What have I done like that? she says, days later when her mother calls. *What she does for those kids,* she says.

They don't know what it is, her mother says.

Could be something they catch, I read. And curious, what I think they said—that we think a disease is something we catch, something lurking when we reach or touch, hiding in wait then suddenly latching when we make the mistake of getting near.

We say, 'we caught a cold,' don't we? the mother says.

As if it couldn't be something we lost, the daughter says. To temptation, maybe, lying in wait, not to reach out to us so much but for us to reach out to it—luring us, diverting us, causing loss as we make our way.

We say, 'we lost our mind,' don't we? the mother says.

Or maybe to bear what we caught or lost is to grasp how little the difference makes, facing what medicine doesn't know. *No one knows,* each of them says.

THE LONG DECEASED BOY'S AILING MOTHER—widowed, infirm, wasted with age, reduced to staring at a TV screen—rarely hears from her younger son, who's divorced, out of work, and sees his daughter when the ex sees fit. Sitting alone in his underwear, a July full moon aloft in the night, he answers a call from Healthwin Center, his mother's skilled-care nursing home. *Weaker,* they tell him, *lucid though.*

A lengthy drive to Healthwin Center, he arranges a stop at his ex's place.

One fish, two fish, he reads to his daughter, then thinks again, as he has before, of the show-and-tell fish a new girl brought to his second-grade class but struggled to speak through a cleft palette that children in class were loath to see. *What would be worse,* he asked a classmate before he knew his brother's plight, *polio or the mouth she's got?* Days later, she didn't come back from a, *Bad, bad cold,* the teacher said, though his instincts told him there had to be more, aggravating untold guilt in him for a cruelty wielded on a helpless child. A child no different from the daughter beside him, awake with congestion and a runny nose, positioning her palette for the *b* and *f*'s to repeat after him, *Red fish, blue fish,* and their usual sign off, *For now, best friend.*

On a night he'd trade for anything else, he continues the drive to his ailing mother, gathers the will to enter the center, knocks on his mother's open door, walks in, sits, and settles to see where the evening goes.

Much like mothers everywhere, she tells him things she's said before. *Too young, you were. You cried so much.*

He looks away.

Then she tells him what he didn't know. *It's happening now. Again,* she says. *Kids who they don't walk no more.* She's quiet for a moment, a passing moment, then she says, *The night.*

Night, he says.

She looks at him as if she knows that nights for him had been unsettling. News of his brother arrived at night—symptoms, worry, prognosis, death—in whispers he'd strain to overhear, often at night from his parents' room. But days back then were filled with light, filled with stories of mischief and wonder in thrillers the Hardy Boys—Frank and Joe—somehow solved, working together, offering adventure and turns-of-chance friends in the neighborhood didn't risk with a boy who might well carry the worst.

Despite the cloud of his brother's absence, he learned to savor what he learned he could. The joy of reading, solitude, a garden in the yard for his mother's plants, the scent of soil on his mother's hands, the faith that this might end—and did.

He thinks of this, all of this.

Leaning in to kiss his mother, not on the face but on her hand, the way he did when she'd dress him up—flannel pants, a hat, a tie, often after his brother was gone—to playact together, just her and him, reliving an era from long ago when a man took a woman by the fingers of her hand to lead her in a fancy dance.

He kisses her hand, not once but twice, erasing for now, if only for now, a summer chill he somehow knows.

Who gets over everything?

Nights

His body drained from the night before, he shirked on cartons packed with product, on windowsills, in vacant stalls. Dozed in an oversized dumbwaiter lift he brought to a stop between two floors. And slept—we're talking deep-rem sleep—by a furnace that raged with flaming heat, feet away from a stack of coal he'd shoveled there himself.

He worked—he did—to get things done, then idled the rest of the grueling shift, his body run-down from sleepless nights plotting to arrange clandestine dens to manage the winter cold. Some knew he'd taken to slacking off, but they also knew his work got done.

They committed to looking after him, to looking the other way.

End of the shift, he punched the clock and walked through snow to the parking lot. Heavier now, the snow had begun at noon, slow. Others rushed to get home quick—meager homes, for sure, but still. He did not rush, or speak, or smile, or look in the direction of those who know. He opened the door, wiped the seat, and sat in the car with his hands by his side with all that was his in the trunk.

Beached on White Sheets

After the carpet ends, she says, voice raised high over dueling laugh tracks, a red-end finger pointing the way. I step past rows of empty gurneys and think again, as I often have, back to the year he came here last, back to the crowded hospital ward, back to the plastic fig tree limb that poked and pierced the white of his eye. And back to the callused hands he raised, one to compress his wounded eye, the other to exact revenge. *Damn fool, you put that here!* he said to my trembling mother, who knew well—we both knew well—to listen up and take it.

The tile—tap, tap—and my bowels tell me I've reached where the voice had said he'd be. I flick stray hair from my shoulder and brow, then look in the room for the bed he's in.

Here is my father, beached on white sheets. Skin droops low on a stroke-stunned face, exaggerating his sunken eye. I sit beside him, eyes to eye. I don't say hello, or smile, or lean. Don't tell him I'm older than he was then. I say, instead, what I came here to say. *My mother wants to see you,* I say. My mouth is parched. My tongue is dry. I inhale deep to catch my breath.

His good eye looks out but not at me. Weak speech comes out—but not to me, towards me—to tell me again, as he had in the past, how he laid new carpet down. *Straight out flat …what I laid,* he says. *No nail holes. No seams.*

I do not know if he knows who I am—or if my voice is reaching him. *She could come,* I say, not saying now. *To visit,* I say, making myself clear to myself.

Nobody laid like me, he says, raising a finger on the hand he can, the other hand limp by the side of a body a sudden stroke left dormant and numb. *A thousand square … on a bad day,* he says. This is my father now, no longer sucking on a glass-bottle teat, dead cells sucking on him.

I look through the room's decorated window, past garland to where my mother waits—inside under the falling snow, covered by the roof of a compact rental, her body warmed by a full-length coat and intermittent sips of lukewarm tea. She cannot see me standing at the window, two floors up from the parking lot. And he can't see my craning eyes, reaching to see her, again now like they did back then.

She's here, I say.

I said, 'I need more … money,' he says, leaning close to spit out more. *Said … 'You want too much,' they said.* The healthy half of his lower lip folds in over toothless gums.

This was not my father then.

Outside, I tell him.

Hell with 'em! my father says, straining to lift his head from the pillow.

I tell him what I want her to want, *To visit.*

You want too much! my father cries, veins popping on his shaven skull, sweat beads dripping from his nose and lip.

In the mirror, I see my thinning hair and, over my shoulder, the red-end finger—curling, curling, one arm pulling, her whole body bent on coaxing me out.

BEFORE THE KOREAN WAR WAS FORGOTTEN, I saw the resentment on my mother's face for the downward spiral in the neighborhood and the split with my father that trapped us there. The last time she let me—the last time I would—I biked at night to my father's walk-up, where the first thing he said was, *Shit's good, have some,* both hands gripping greasy chicken, bloodshot eyeball focused.

I nodded. That was all I did.

Shoot tomorrow? my father asked.

Sure, I said like a kid's supposed to, my stomach weak from the sight of him biting, the sound of him belching, the smell of glue on his carpet layer clothes, and the ring of sweat in his armpits.

We'll shoot at the dump then, early, he said. *Won't yet stink then, early.*

In the foggy morning's available light, he paired his work boots side by side, then pulled them up and on slowly, his thick hands skilled in the ways of means. He let me handle a .45 caliber handheld pistol he'd snuck in a duffle from the Imjin River, where his company's captain—*A weak kneed coward,* my father said—deserted the platoon, eighteen boys to fend for themselves, enemy lines approaching in numbers, reinforcements a half day away.

He carried the pistol to the car himself and let me carry a target rifle, the only gun I've ever fired—but not that day and not thereafter, not after the shot he fired that day.

We left the car in an empty lot, climbed a broken, splintered fence, and walked toward the dump site, guns in hand.

Stalking, not talking, just like seasoned soldiers would.

Shh..., my father whispered, watching, his eye set straight to a distant spot. He raised the pistol and fired once. Rather than the squeal of a rat distressed, the scream of a human voice shot back. Branches cracked under falling weight.

We ran to a spot where a boy fell limp, thick blood gushing from the base of his neck. My father said, *Say what I tell you*—and he didn't tell me to say much. *Say you were looking the other way. Didn't see a thing, say.*

Later at a wake where the body lay, I kneeled by the boy, like others did. *To pay our respects,* my father said. *To cover his ass,* my mother said. I looked at the boy's face, soul-silent, and a collar around where blood had gushed. We didn't stay long but long enough. We walked from the casket, from a weeping mother, from an angry facescape glad we left.

And my father walked when the charges were dropped.

What mattered most when the fuss died down had little to do with a bullet to the neck. The long serving District Attorney—*A candy ass,* my mother said—served for a time on the Imjin River.

I STEP-TAP THROUGH THE HOSPITAL ENTRANCE—out the door, down the steps—my full weight balanced on a tripod cane, just like the clinical therapist said. *In a rhythm like this,* the therapist said, standing up to show me how. *Step, tap, step; step, tap, step.*

I clear the windshield's gathering snow and look at my mother, who's looking out, smiling at what she can see of me. I step back, linger, catch my breath, and think back to the day the fig tree came, to her lively joy carrying it in, to her fingers caressing faux-silk leaves—then pressing later on blood that spilled from her mangled nose and mouth.

I pull—both hands—on the car door handle, toss the cane behind the seat, and lift my leg to enter. The cabin is soaked in the stale scent of cheap perfume fermenting. Here is my mother. Belted, sipping, fighting the daily fight to right a crimp that stoops her spine.

There is silence in the car—a moment of ever-so-rare silence—that ends again when she starts again, nearly this time where she left off before, reshaping past plot lines of long ago (*Too young, you were,* she'd say to me), exaggerating details of an imagined youth (*Hallmark stole the inscriptions I sent*), fabricating dead men haunted by her charm (*You can tell,* she'd say in a way I'd rather not hear from her).

This is my mother now, running on the engines of memory and loss. And this was my mother then.

Wasn't as bad as I heard, I interrupt.

My mother turns to look at me. *What?* she says. *Oh, how'd she look?*

Pale … I cough. *Drawn,* I say.

I drive the car to the toll road exit, struggle for my wallet to pay the toll, and retrace the rest of the route to her house—a billboard, corners, street signs, lights. *Route checks,* she says, *to the avenue,* she calls it, like everyone calls Branch Avenue, a fourth-generation mixed use neighborhood resisting the transition from middle class to the full-on threat of blight.

She wipes her lips with her fingertips. She peers through her glasses, the windshield, the snow, forward to where we're driving now and back to where she's always been.

She'll recover? she asks. *The woman will?*

I look at my mother. *It's routine today.*

You knew her from where?

School, I say.

The wind is fierce, a howling tempest of energy. I lean-in over the steering wheel, into the wipers' swish-and-thump.

How'd it happen? my mother asks.

Stress, I guess. Who knows, I say.

We ride the white road. Cars in a line. Snow falling. A few cars passing, some cars stopped.

Little flakes, my mother says. *Little flakes, big snow* … I half see the road. … *big flakes, little snow,* I hear her say.

I don't see the road. I see red blurs.

My mother says something I can't quite hear.

THUMP to the front, *WHACK* to the back. We are framed by bent fenders, encased in a swirl of blinding white. It is not day; it is not night. I am sinking, falling, fading.

It is black.

NOT LONG AFTER THE YOUNG BOY'S FUNERAL, I caught a baseball square in the eye, passed-out briefly, and came-to clammy, confused, and cold. Driving with my mother to the hospital, I sat in the front seat rigid and scared, holding an icepack over my brow, wanting to tell her what I'd been thinking.

I've been thinking, I said to my mother.

Sure, she said, looking ahead.

I feel different, I said. Sweat beads formed on my brow and lips, my heart thumped deep and quickened.

You got a good bump.

No.

And the shooting will take time.

No.

You'll be okay, you'll see, you will. They'll give you something, she said to me, one hand griping the steering wheel, the other aligning a sagging icepack I held tight on my injured eye. *Hold it close as you can,* she said. *Close as you can stand,* she said.

This wasn't what I'd been thinking.

At the hospital, a doctor aimed a penlight toward my eye. He touched the bulge on my swollen brow, squinted, and looked in close at my eye. *What happened?* the doctor asked.

I was heading home …

Your home?

Home plate, I said.

No one did this? he asked.

What?

Hit you?

I was startled. These aren't questions they ask a rich kid. Not from what my mother said.

WE ARE BOTH ADMITTED, MY MOTHER AND ME. She is released soon thereafter, the seatbelt having constrained her well. I am held for the coming night, one floor below where my father lies.

We'll need to see, a doctor says, *if a temperature spikes or fatigue sets in.*

A temperature spikes, fatigue sets in.

I wake up to tubes, a monitor, and the ebb and flow of game show applause.

My mouth, now, is unusually dry.

My mother's aging balloon knuckle fingers comb my fallen hair back. Leaning, she reaches for the call button laying on the mattress aside my head. *Good they kept you,* she says to me. *Kept you here,* she says.

I look at my mother's eyes close up and make the startling reconciliation from the clear bright eyes that raised me alone to the gray-white shade of her eyes now. Some of the pigment in the white of her eyes matches the roots of her colored hair.

The door opens. A new set of fingers enters the room, then disappears into surgical gloves—this time not pointing or curling or pulling but probing deep at my stomach and chest. She turns me over onto my stomach. The fingers dig at my buttocks and back.

I turn my head to look at her. My stomach tightens.

Discomfort? the doctor asks.

Pain, I say.

We'll need your records, she says to me. *You're not from here?*

Was, I say. *Been away for years.*

My mother's mouth repeats, *Your records.* She moves in closer—closer to the bed. She rubs the sweat from my neck and chest and brings to her lips two fingertips.

He comes back, my mother says, touching my temple briefly, softly, just like she did when I was a kid.

I force a smile.

My mother's smile lines curl on her cheeks, then fall lower till they're almost down.

The gloved fingers on the doctor's hand whisk long hair that's fallen past one of her ears, making its way toward open lips that barely move as she whispers to me. *What have they told you?* the doctor asks—part knowing, part probing, leaning close so my mother won't hear.

On my stomach, I turn my head toward the doctor, pause, then part my lips to speak. I don't tell her neglect formed lumps in my lungs or my time left, if timed right, is less than I hoped. I don't tell her what's failed, what's failing, what's feigned, who's passed on, who's left now, who's gone. I instead tell a tale spun tall for my mother and leave out what everyone knows.

Isn't It Better That She Knows?

Me? You think you're kidding me? Hey, this is David. Remember me? I'm the one who first fell for your diversions. I'm the one you kept from telling what you showed me. What you showed me!

And little did I know what you'd show anybody, including what you let fall out in front of my father—yeah, that's right, *my* father—before conniving him out of whatever it was you were conniving him out of. The man you called "father" for God's sake!

This isn't about your hand. Like hell it is! This is about your chance to claim your fortune—with the very same hand you used to endorse the checks I sent for what you called matters of life or death. *I can't say for what. I can't tell you why.* I'll tell you why you can't say for what! Look, you meant little to me in childhood, less later, and nothing now in middle age. Do you hear me? Nothing! I don't want to see you. I don't want to know you. I don't want to know anything about you.

Are you listening to me?

Are you listening to me tell you that in the years since you last saw fit to call me, I've not spent even so much as one minute of my time thinking about you fondly. Fondly, I said. Did you hear me say fondly? Which is to say, I haven't thought of you lovingly in years!

Do you hear me? Don't you dare call me again. And don't, for God's sake, call me this pompous shit name you call me, "David." Never the name your mother called me. Oh, no. Never the name of anybody that might divert attention from your view of what others might view as the importance of the person named.

Robert, not Bob. Charles, not Charlie, even though no one called Charles Petteruti anything other than Charlie, except for the people who called him names. And speaking of names, I'll tell you the name!

How Much I Must Have Looked
Like Her to Her

I could see that my mother was motionless, limp, her face held up in my father's hands. Her uncovered belly was paper thin, not at all like it seemed like a mother's should be.

You been here? he asked, looking at her, but talking to me.

Since school, I said. *Haven't been out.* I was a child who stayed in the house, tucked-in even in the light of day. *Homework,* I said. *Math,* I said. This was in the year that letters meant numbers, a time when my voice was a sign of change.

Who was it? he asked, turning toward me.

I lifted an arm—in case.

Dark as the shade of fertile dirt, his eyes looked up and at me. He dropped my mother's face. He reached for my face. *Who was here? Who was it?* he said, eyes peering, nose holes flaring, chin skin puckered like a turkey's wattle.

These hands I was held in were roofer's hands—hardened, callused, sandpaper rough. A finger, stumped by an errant saw, dug in hard at the side of my face. Rough on me, he was gentle with her. Shouldn't it be the other way around?

I don't know. I don't! I said, not knowing that a lie has a sound of its own.

The pressure of his finger on my cheek was full-willed. I'd felt the weight of his will before. I'd been within an inch of my life before. I faced him—arm up—thinking again, like I had before. What God would give this man a life seven times longer than a dog's?

You know, you do, he said to me, his black hair bluer than a dead crow mounted on the end of a high chief's dancing stick.

No! I answered, head locked, lying. I loved to say the word "no" as a child. "No" was tactile, forceful, bold in a way that "yes" was anything else. These are things that therapists teach when a mother tells them, *He doesn't talk.*

Toward her, he turned my color-stained face. On the nightstand was a candle with a speechless flame—the tongue, I thought, of an absent mother. I did not want him to turn me toward her. I wanted from him the last great gift that a parent gives to a waiting child. The gift of his one last final breath.

Look at her, he said to me. *Look at her,* he said again. There was weight to his hands and power in his voice, then power in his hands and weight to his voice. This was the way my father would get to the sense he thought he was making.

Maybe before I got home, I told him. *Before I got home from school,* I said, hoping to turn his attention from me.

Look, he said, releasing his hold.

Look? Really, he said that to me? Everything in me that had to do with knowing, I knew from having looked at her. The expressions on her face were my first form of language, her eyes my first unspoken code, her midriff the source of the mark on my skin.

Look, he repeated, pointing. *Lookit!*

I looked at her.

This was my mother, after all. Or before all.

My mother was lying in a drugged-up stupor, unaware that her robe had opened at the waist. Her face was a blurred moon, puffed up and pasty, her cheeks a cold milk yellow. One eye turned in in its wayward way; the other looked vacant, rolled-over white, having gotten that way—that vacant-white way—when a needle was stuck in her forearm or leg.

But more that day, *more* vacant that day, *more* rolled-over white—*more, more* on any of the days a man came to stick a needle in her skin.

I'm in a way with myself, she'd say to me when she thought she owed me an explanation.

Dad, I whispered, my young head angled to tell him—remind him?—that I was a product of my mother's sins. My way was a matter of manner and form that rarely told truths to anyone else, especially him on the rare occasion—an occasion like this—when I thought it best to say "dad" to him, rather than what I'd say to myself.

He did not know the pass whisper. He did not even know what I came to know. You don't touch the mother of your best friend's kid.

Out in the open, I said to my father. *Right here,* I said. *The door left open.*

He pulled me in with both his hands to offer the wisdom of a tribal elder. *No one like her cares what you think.*

This was the way with my father. What he said about her said more about him.

Tell me, he said. *Just tell me who.*

Language has a way of revealing itself in the ear of a child who has learned to listen. To me, what he said when he said "just tell" was "tell me and I won't knock you silly." We usually talked halfway between us, but this had pulled me too far near unspeakable truths about my mother and a wallop from my furthest-most next of kin.

Why could he not set the world out before me and then just get out of the way? Isn't that the way?

A man? I said. *I was up in my room, my room,* I said, this time not lying—or entirely lying—but my bowels told me, don't tell him more. Don't tell him this happened more often than he knew, that when it did, her body was exposed, and then when it was, I hid in the hall to peek in one-eyed to see what she did. From there in the hall, I was thoroughly her creature, watching her breaths, some hurried, some not. From there, I could see reflected in the mirror that my mother had a mark, a stain the color of red-brown wine, born on my mother and bred onto me below the bone where bent hair grows in the form of a lifeform, formed like a leaf.

Surely, she knows.

Surely, she's seen the mark on me.

Outside, the wind blew upside down, spitting in drifts a sideways rain I'd have hidden from—alone, if I could—if it weren't for what he was asking me.

Who? he said. *Who?!* he demanded.

I looked at my mother, lying limp. I could see that there is a hell and that she will get there.

SO LIBERATING WHEN THE MIND WANDERS. The face erases all sign of phrasing and nothing on the body puts on airs. No vanity, pretense, or cunning ploy and all that awaits is suspended in time. These are the moments—rare at first, common at last—when guarded demeanor relaxes fully, dissolving obsessive worry and fear. A blessing this happens when it comes to happen, delivering me to a comforting truth. Who we are, is when we're alone.

I CLIMB INTO BED, A LEG AT A TIME, the wind and rain howling outside. The sheets smell clean, freshly laundered, hinted with the scent of a perfumed softener. My wife smells clean, freshly showered, her long hair set in place just so.

Okay? she asks.

I am turned to the side, my head backed-up to a face marked-up with drawn-on lines that concede to age. I ignore what she says. I do not flinch. First among the powers of silence is peace.

Are you? she asks.

I do not answer.

This is my wife. She is every wife. She is everywhere there is inside this house that I live in now and lived in then. She is dripping from the faucets, rattling in the blinds, howling in the furnace, tapping on the pipes. She is everywhere there is, even where the full-length mirror was.

Why don't you ... she begins, *tell me?* she asks.

Sweat beads mount in hair I shade to my mother's color where it did not show. The silence is monotonous, rhythmic, pounding, and marked as it is by what marks time—tick-tock, breathing, the beat of my heart. I roll onto my back. I will go that far. Maybe an involuntary act will follow.

Why don't you talk? she says to me. *Talk to me. Talk when this happens.*

A dim light falls from a bedside clock. Squinting, I can see on the table by the clock an unlit lamp and an address book that lists most of my mother at the end of the M's and the overflow about her over onto N. I shut my eyes, but I can see—if only in my mind's eye, I can see. The lazy eye turns in an oddly, off centered, overcompensated imbalance that photos captured but my mother tried to hide. When the eye turned in, her face turned to right it—in what looked like to me like a turn too far.

Why do I see this at times like this—these too often times when I see again what I saw back then when a man stuck a needle into her skin? She'd raise her head, nostrils bloating, and shoulder-roll her cover-up down to the sheet, exposing what I could not bear to see. Elliptical cutlines twirled on fake skin, marking the borders where plastic met flesh, both breasts knife marked, the fake tips brown, a mass of what flesh on dying becomes. Slowly, she'd rub where the needle went in—massaging one way, or the other, or both—driving her lazy eye out and in.

Each move brought her, *Closer,* she'd say—quietly, maybe, or right out loud—to a place that seemed confusing to me. There is pressure in my bowels, a sound, and seeping—all, I can tell, from what I am thinking.

My wife dabs my cheek with the tips of her fingers, cycling in circles below my eye. There is touching between us, then something, some gaining, some willingness to speak. Why does the mind fail to admit what the body knows as the utter truth?

There, she says. *There, there,* she says.

Her eyelids flutter in a brief but unspoken, unambiguous code that announces again who she shouldn't be.

Her.

Yes, her.

My mother, her!

She has roots in my mother but as weeds have roots. Like my mother, she's learned from living with me that loneliness is a cruelty only hinted at by death.

She looks at my face, both eyes focused like my mother's couldn't.

Okay, she whispers in the wifely way she always had.

I do not know the pass whisper. I know only that this should look like it matters, like I faked it to look when my father died.

She blots damp sweat with a back swipe of liver spots on hands that have labored to live with me. With both hands, she rakes back long, flowing hair, then does tonight what my mother had done. Her head turns, her lids slit, her eyes check the time.

Try as I have, I don't turn away. Try as I might, I can't turn away. There is a way that whatever I turn away from turns out in time to own me. This is the way, was always the way, even when I acted like I could not speak.

I lay still for my wife with my hands on the mark that I came to learn my mother had too. This time, like last time, will pass away in time. In the meantime, this time, I shut my eyes to hear this house at every wind on the siding, on the roof, from the wailing rain.

Their Version

The wife leans in to tell me the worst part. *The footsteps! So creepy. You don't think. You run.* Her hand grips a nightgown high on her neck.

The husband says, *You run!* There is bare leg below the hem of his coat, a compression wrap above his foot. *Right over here,* I think he says. The healthy side of his shaven face has no more expression than the palsied side.

I drop my bag at the foot of the bed.

Took a picture? I ask.

Had it when he ran, she says.

He ran? I ask.

His fingers tap a zoom-lens camera. Her fingers cling to her nightgown top.

Saw nothing? I ask.

Well … there was a car, my wife says.

The husband and the wife look at my wife. Then they look at me. *Yes,* they say, almost together.

You saw it? I ask my wife.

Heard it, she says.

Description? I ask.

Of what? my wife asks.

What you heard.

Right, she says. *A muffler,* she says.

Before they got here? I ask my wife.

Of course, she says. *Then you came in.*

There's rouge on her cheeks, liner on her lids, and her lips are painted to match the lids.

Cancelled? she asks.

Delayed, I say. *Connection had left.*

I look at them. Each one of them close. If I didn't know that his face had fallen, I'd say their faces all looked the same.

The Card Catalog

The father is sitting, a Camel in hand, browsing the afternoon paper. The mother is sitting, sleeves rolled up, sewing a coat and a service patch a reunion demands the father wear. Later they'll turn to *The Lucy Show*, but for now their ears are tuned to the door and to word of war on the evening news.

The son, seventeen, opens the door carrying an outsized stack of books, all but one wrapped in contact paper and fastened tight in a leather belt, just like a kid at school does. Home on time was good for the boy. Hair trimmed tight was good for the boy. Not hearing his name was good, too.

The father adjusts a bean bag ashtray, rests the paper on aching knees, then turns his attention to the mother and the boy. It's sometimes good for the mother and the boy when the father pays attention to them.

The mother stands, needle in hand, eyes directed to the young boy's eyes then down to the books in the leather belt. *Get what you needed?* she asks the boy, eyeing the unwrapped book. There's little expression on the mother's face and none apparent on the father's face, not counting one eye's thyroid bulge and the other's squint through cigarette smoke.

The boy says, yes, like the trooper he is, but offers no detail. Instead, he unbuckles the leather belt, removes from the stack a dark green book, and raises the book in his outstretched hand toward where his mother and father sit. The mother can see, or thinks she sees, rectangles bordering a three-line title, all in capital letters. She figures the book is what he needed—the one unadorned in contact paper—but she gets to the book in a roundabout way.

From the library? the mother asks.

Right, he says.

Mrs. Pollitt help? the mother asks.

No, but she said to say, 'Hello.'

She's so nice, the mother says. Neither the boy nor the father says a word. *That book what you needed?* the mother asks.

It is, yeah, the boy answers.

The father stands, cigarette in hand, and removes his half-rim reading glasses.

She didn't help? the mother asks.

I didn't ask, the boy says. *The card catalog. Found it there.*

She looks at him like a mother would. The blank expression on her face makes clear she thinks he's hiding something—or if he isn't, then holding back, just like a lot of kids his age. Rare was the teen, then as now, who failed to shade the truth. Not so much a lie, so much, but to keep the barrage of questions at bay. The parents suspect he shades the truth—the father more than the mother does. Nothing they can put their finger on, since most of what they've witnessed lately is accompanied by silence. Unthinkable then—not now, then—was the teen who'd even dare to tell what they're thinking about inside.

Funny how parents think of things and don't see the kids are thinking too.

Got it for class, the boy offers.

What is it? the father asks.

William S. Burroughs, the boy says.

Means nothing to me, the father says. *What's it called? The book.*

Let's see, the boy says out loud, knowing full well the title of the book—he'd looked up the book by author and title—but alert that confusion diverts attention, if not the suspicion his parents had. Turning the book with both his hands, he pulls the cover closer. *The Naked Lunch,* he reads out loud.

What? the mother says to the boy.

Naked? the father says to himself.

A novel with chapters the teacher said the author said, 'You can read in any order you want.'

The father and the mother look at the boy, but the boy avoids both sets of eyes. He's been through this with them before. Doubtful, probing, expressive stares that translate often to disapproval or a sly staging to ask him more.

Mr. Merrill, the boy says. *He said that.*

Merrill, the mother says.

Said what? the father asks.

Read it in any order, the boy says. *The chapters, in any order you want and talk about it in class, then.*

The father knew and the mother knew that this was a lot for the boy to say.

The father and the mother were suspicious of the teacher. A funny feeling, both of them. Enough to discuss between themselves, though not with anyone else—so far. The father, first when he overheard that the teacher hadn't served. *Not even the bloody Reserves,* he'd said. And the mother, later when she saw by chance that the teacher wasn't wearing socks at an evening parent-teacher event. *Beatnik?* the mother said at the time. *In front of the kids in the day, I guess?* Nothing to report, neither of them. Not on Merrill so far, there wasn't, but more than enough to bide their time, keep a searching eye on him, and speak up when there was enough—like they did with the young unmarried teacher, working nights as a cocktail waitress, wearing skirts up to her butt and tops that showed off everything. They'd speak-up again with enough on him.

The bottom of this is what they were after. But first to the bottom of what they'd call a book, "No good could come from."

Each one made a mental note of what they thought the boy had said. "Burrow," they thought, or something like that. And "Naked Lunch"—*that* they got. Neither could see the cover close, and neither would chance seizing the book, held tight in one of the boy's hands. Too untrusting, they both knew, even though they wanted to. The mother would try to read what she could—in a bookstore, say, if she found the time. Or maybe explore with Mrs. Pollitt, a polished, well-read library staple who women in town admired so, partly for her manner and enviable looks but mostly for an inherited wealth that allowed her to volunteer her time. If only the mother could look at the book. To get an idea, to size it up, without risking the disapproval of the library's arbitress of culture.

Really? the father says to the boy. *What kind of book do you read out of order, if the book's supposed to be good for kids?* Saying "kids" to the boy was risky, coming from a father the boy knew was intent on making a man of his son.

Supposed to buy it, the boy says, *but no one checked it out yet. Figured I'd save on buying the book.*

Good for you! the father says of a move the young boy understood could change the subject, if nothing else, and make his father proud of him. A high school halfback, Phi Beta Kappa, and a long-ago veteran of foreign wars, the father was always on high alert to work his boorish experiences in. *Both ways, we went—both sides of the ball. This is a conflict—that was war.* The boy struggled to make him proud. Grades, church, mowing the lawn, plans with a kid whose accomplished father the boy's father admired. "Good for you" was good for now.

That it? the mother asks the boy, whose back he now had turned toward them. *Just for the book, that book, you went?*

The boy returns the book to the stack and fastens the belt around them, erasing the mother's dwindling hope to peruse the book without him. *Yeah,* he says, *the book, that's right,* but keeps to himself what he couldn't say. The card catalog—at least through N—had nothing on what he couldn't ask a blabber-mouth librarian for.

Two-Thirty

In school, I tell you, it wasn't safe to let kids know the work made sense. Not in the school that I was in. You wouldn't get bullied or worse at first, but you would get puzzled, threatening looks. The better move was misdirection, like a well-timed crack that mocked a teacher. "Who's bra?" for algebra; "diaphragm" for a diagrammed sentence. Wise, I learned, to make a crack under your breath that appealed to the kids' carnal longings but not so often—this was the trick—that you drew attention from the tougher kids. Smart in school wasn't smart among the kids fully adept in the ways of streetwise navigation. Why pay when you can steal quicker or settle a check when no one's looking? It didn't add up to them.

Street-smart pays was the tough kids' way, implying to us, the rest of us, that book smart should be punished. And that's where my problem was. I hid from kids that I liked to read, welcomed term-long science projects, understood the math we did, and considered a highlight of each school year a trip to the Philharmonic. Any of these would have been enough, more than enough, to put the tough kids on my case. Take the boy, the studious one, who announced an error in a teacher's math and was lucky to get off heckled.

In the year that grades got more precise—plus, minus, and in between—I thought that kids were catching on, presenting for me an alarming risk. Fewer laughed at my smart-aleck quips, including the toughest, Joe Bondanza, known for beating his father silly and making his uncle say "uncle" out loud before releasing the poor man's head. Bondanza was new to our public school but a well-known menace, nevertheless.

Trouble was, he was staring at me and took to holding his shoulders stiff when I walked by or near him. This was the first ominous sign, the first unspoken warning. Minor maybe, if it isn't you, but no one messed with Joe Bondanza—still I shudder when I say his name!—lest he say, finger in your chest, the dreaded "two-thirty." That's all he'd say, *Two-thirty*. That was enough. Enough notice, no exceptions, to meet Bondanza after school where, surrounded by a pack of kids, he'd beat you up bare handed. Rumor had it he'd beat you less if you gave no sign of fighting back. A rumor because no one saw, other than the toughest kids—and none of them would say. Not unless Bondanza said, and he wasn't one to talk.

Most kids took it standing straight, both hands down, submissive. No sense getting beaten worse. The ones who didn't, paid.

There was something brewing in the air between us. Me and Joe Bondanza.

I was in a fix of my own making, partly for too many smart-aleck cracks, but mostly for first-term final grades due in the office soon. None of the kids would share their grades—not what kids would do back then—but the damned school posted an Honor Roll on a bulletin board outside the gym. Anyone could see. Any of the streetwise kids could see. Problem was, I was cruising toward a string of As—*all* As, highest honors—which would place my name at the top of the roll, the worst possible place to be. In the mix for smartest kid in the school and the crosshairs of Joe Bondanza, who just last year at another school beat up the school's salutatorian, the valedictorian having been a girl.

He was good about that, girls.

I needed a way to evade Bondanza. A way to get a last-minute D to prevent achieving highest honors and ditch me from the Honor Roll. Turns out a D would pass the course, but even just a single D would rule out any honors, despite my grades in everything else. One D would do the job and wouldn't be that hard to achieve, since rumor had it that no one submitting a poster board—a board with something relevant on it— would be denied at least a D. A low bar but who's complaining? I had to submit enough for a D and hope for nothing higher.

There had to be a way.

There was a way—a deceptive, devious, calculating way to get me off the hook. Rather than submit a science project teachers would expect of me—like the time-travel poster I'd already done weeks before the project was due—I plotted a scheme to head-off the kids, mostly Joe Bondanza. I figured science was broad enough to capture how things worked. We studied locomotion, didn't we? I needed a project in the broad contours of, say, science-at-work that would remove the prospect of teachers deciding I needed to submit another. Just enough, but not too much. A balancing act, for sure.

A second chance for a promising student wasn't what I wanted. I risked a beating. And from a kid who everyone knew—kids, teachers, the office too—wouldn't submit a project at all. Everyone risked a beating. Ask the teacher at his last school who pressed charges in criminal court, sued the school in civil court, and left the profession soundly defeated—the cases having been dismissed—raising the suspicion for all who'd follow that Bondanza knew someone, someone knew him, or everyone knew to stand clear.

No way around it, I needed a D. No adult could help with this.

I abandoned the project I had completed and removed the face of an old gear-clock that hung on our landlord's cellar wall. The clock hadn't worked in my lifetime and wasn't something a landlord would miss. I removed the facing, clamped the gears to a poster board, and wrote at the top in magic marker, "The Internal Workings of a Clock." That was it. Nothing more, but credibly within my definition of science-at-work and likely sufficient to misdirect a teacher expecting more from me.

It was.

I got the grade I knew would work, secured my secret from the streetwise kids, fended for now Bondanza's scorn, and not only put my problem to rest but brought to an irreversible end my teachers' long held faith in me.

What were you thinking? the teacher asked.

A step back, no? a counselor said to the teacher about my thinking.

I was reprieved, no problem there, Bondanza's shoulders lenient and limp in the hall outside the gym, where I came to think—right then, right there—that maybe I'd lost my sense of proportion in the face of a risk I'd overthought, only to find that the risk I dodged wasn't the one before me.

Angst

I turn to the board, reach for chalk, and sneak a peek at my watch. The disbelief is plain on my face. It's got to be, I'm sure. But I hold out hope that no one noticed, distracted as undergraduates are. A term-to-term adjunct instructor is much beholden to the whims of kids—and kids to the optics in view before them. *Customer satisfaction,* the chair had said, announcing part of the moving target my renewal would depend on.

I stretch the material I had prepared on Elizabeth Bishop's "In the Waiting Room," the last of the day's assigned readings. I'd read the poem as a high school kid—found myself astonished—and then produced, years later, a thesis on her body of work. I vowed back then that, were I blessed, I'd name a daughter Elizabeth. Not only because I worshiped her verse and several of her stories, but also because her published letters reveal a shy, guarded demeanor that presented to her closer friends like I present to mine—open with her intimates but otherwise shy.

Guarded and shy is me all over.

A mysterious poem, an insightful poem, "Waiting Room" invites a reader to relive the moment it dawned on them that they're a wholly unique being, separate and distinct from everyone else. Who doesn't face the epiphany Bishop brings to bear? I am *me,* you are *not,* and the body I'm in is *different!*

I marvel at the thought of this looking out from the body I'm in.

I recite the poem out loud in class, repeat aloud some telling lines—*you are an I ... nothing stranger had ever happened ... could ever happen*—then lob a question to the class. *You've all felt that—have you not? At some point in your life?*

No one takes the bait. Not one.

Worse, glancing down at my watch, I'm panicked to see I've come to this—the end of what I'd planned to say—with little left to fill the time remaining in the class. The early, noon, and afternoon classes, none with more than several enrolled, ended in triumph with a host of comments, all spot-on to Bishop's poem. Particularly the afternoon class, when moments before the end of class, a startled student raised her hand, stood up tall, and announced, *Not till now, I hadn't!* Leaving class, no few students gathered around my podium to continue the volley of apt comments that delivered a fitting close.

But in this class, the late day oversubscribed class, neither a volley nor a remark. I'm out of gas too early.

Two more vignettes is all I've got—one from Bishop's memoirs, another from her letters—both of which I was tickled to discover but cut from my thesis to stay within a none-too-lenient page count limit. I'm hopeful the two will do the trick, not to propel them to the edge of their seats— not this crowd, not this term—but to get this class to the end of class without releasing the class too early, voices raised, doors slamming, drawing the attention of nearby faculty, all of whom are senior to me, each with the clout to do me in.

I may be blowing this out of proportion, but the customer isn't the student only. There's also the faculty in my midst and some of them, I've come to imagine, would leap to turn their mother in.

I refer them first to *The Country Mouse*, a Bishop memoir I hadn't assigned but could pay-off in a way more potent than merely arriving at the end of class. Might students mention my resourcefulness in end of term evaluations? This is my largest section, by far. A lot to ask—for them to mention—but students have in the past, I know. Takes just one to make the claim for a department chair to notice.

I tell the students the memoir reveals that the poem relives Bishop as a six-year-old, accompanying to the dentist on a winter day her dear Aunt Jenny. On arrival, Aunt Jenny handed Bishop from a waiting room pile a 1918 *National Geographic* that figures in the poem. It never does good to explain too much; it's better for students to discover for themselves. *Socratic learning,* the chair had said; "critical thinking," the syllabus read. But for one thing, I need to fill the time and, for another, I need the approval of teens to win another contract renewal.

And I want this job, I do.

For many, it's not a job to want—cut-rate wage, no health insurance. For me, the very job I want, since it discounts faculty children's tuition—*A recruiting tool,* the chair had said—even for an adjunct's kid. In my case, my Elizabeth, an applicant to the first-year class.

The Country Mouse doesn't land. True as it is, it doesn't land.

I spot a yawn, a slouch in the back, and some of them napping or fully distracted or fumbling through their wretched things. I resort to lobbing a toss-up question. *Has anyone experienced the insight that the young girl in the poem does?* No bites, no stirs, few upright faces. In vain, I ask, *Do you, Elizabeth?*

Looking as if she'd been disturbed, she gives no sign she appreciates the irony of my calling on her. She's my daughter, for God's sake, sitting in the room at my insistence, an entrée to a college class well before the fall.

A lifeline from my daughter, maybe?

No, she says, head held down, pissed I allow no phones in class, telling me—I know this girl—that the burden to answer is on the enrolled, certainly not on a high school kid. She doesn't blurt, *You're asking me?* Or, *Let's get something straight.* But both are written all over her face. More important—for the moment, at least—there's nothing in anyone's body language to suggest that either my voice or demeanor signaled to them my growing angst.

I'm in a pickle of my own making but maybe it's not apparent yet.

I take them next to a Bishop letter, written decades after the poem, a confession of sorts to Frank Bidart, accomplished poet and life-long friend. Naming names is good, I figure, particularly the name of a living writer whose work I hadn't assigned in class, offering the chance to appear connected and doubling as a reminder of my advanced taste.

The New Yorker having accepted the poem, Bishop—daunted that the magazine's fact-checking engine—reveals in the letter she walked in terror to the New York Public Library to confirm the February 1918 number was the *National Geographic* from which she adopted images prominent in the poem: riding breeches, naked women, rivulets of fire and ash thrown from a volcano. She checks each image, one by one, and finds that she was partly wrong, poetic license notwithstanding. Much like me, she panics.

Imagine a poet of great promise feeling compelled to cover her tracks? Imagine that! I say again, this time pitching my voice farther—my sometimes tool to garner attention—biding my time, diverting them, then telling them that, rather than walk, *I'm sure I would have run to the library!*

Some eyes open, some heads rise, but nothing more than that.

I'm cooked.

Granted, asides are beside the point, irrelevant musings designed to achieve little more than a timely end of class. But these are students, undergrads, and don't all students revel in delight in the face of a teacher's extraneous asides, confident asides will not be tested? Vignettes exhausted—and repeated in paraphrase at least once each—I swallow hard, pause in place, fake a smile, and plot my turn toward the analog clock, perched on the wall behind my back, hoping the wall clock's minute hand has pulled ahead of my watch.

It's my only hope.

No way to access the blasted clock other than a full half-turn to the clock. I've planned for this, inching toward it step by step. A turn away, I start to turn, then stop, then turn, brushing the corner of the podium, arousing the notice of a number of students, even my Elizabeth. Piercing eyes, an edgy smirk, disturbed for the second time today, she's unaware—how could she be?—that waiting alone in a crowded room, anticipation setting in, no measure of angst is more than it is before the end of the angst is near.

The Body Double of Making Do

We acknowledged signs on Michael's face through eye talk, nods, and silent glances until the night Kay found her nerve. *They'd help him now, I think*, she said, *if tests they got could tell.* My appetite stalled in the frightful days after a battery of tests was done, awaiting results but dreading calls, ignoring the appearance of Michael's eyes—crossed, heavy, beet red lids—and the mucus caked on curly lashes Kay once called, *a woman's dream.*

The doctor told us, *Down, mosaic. Not severe, not profound*—but didn't say what mosaic meant or why it's not profound. The words were largely new to me but came alive days later when I saw a boy in a fast-food line, up on his toes, hands dangling beneath his chin, lips struggling to form a word in the shadow of his mother's quiet calm and the smile that masked my face.

Kay soon folded inside of herself, into the abyss I'd been resisting, returning at times to say odd things—*Should we tell him? Does he know?*—becoming a mere third person reference in my and Michael's first-person world. Why is that so often the way with the one you hoped to lean on?

MICHAEL WAS WITH ME WHEN I WAS FREE—nights, weekends, holidays. But he wasn't one day weeks later when he had a spell of high-speed rage and low-pitched grunting that neighbors heard through open windows we'd hurry to shut when we thought of it. He slammed screen doors, grunted, jumped, and screamed with fury at the top of his lungs, terrifying Kay when he reached for her and surprising me when I walked in. What could I do to calm my boy, pants unbuttoned and riding low, transformed at dusk like a werewolf would?

It happens. It does. It <u>*has*</u>, Kay said, flailing her arms like Michael does.

He does this often? the doctor asked.

She nodded up and down, *Yes. But more when he's seen me,* she said. I looked at her. She looked away.

We could have told the doctor more. Instead, I said, *Can Down do that?*

Could, yes, the doctor said. *But could be just blood sugar too. What does he see?* the doctor asked, *Between you two at home.*

Kay looked down, didn't speak. The doctor, standing, looked at me. *Normal stuff,* I said.

You're patient with him? the doctor asked.

Much as we can, I said back, ignoring the days of frightful nights when I screamed louder than Michael did. Kay didn't look at the doctor or me.

The doctor licked her upper lip. *I know,* she said, *now listen.* She said we needed qualified help, but not the kind where therapists visit—an option I'd been angling for. Rather, the kind where Michael's admitted, maybe even permanently. She recommended Lanning Center, a state run home—a term that rang untrue to me—that black-shawled matrons in the neighborhood mocked in dismissive facial gestures to punctuate their old world speech. *Abbandono,* I'd heard them say, often about a neighbor kid. Abandoned, shuttered, left to fend.

I didn't like where this was heading. "Lock him up" it sounded to me. *No,* I said, *Me, myself, I'll care for him.* That wasn't what I wanted to say. I wanted to say "we" instead but said what I knew I needed to say.

We talked skilled care and public aid—the doctor about it, me around it—then the doctor pulled us in. *You're raising a child, you can't at home.* I knew she knew things closed to us, but I didn't expect she'd come so quick to the clarifying moment of Michael's fate.

Driving back from admitting Michael—far too soon for my taste—I felt a brief reprieve, like owning-up to a crime you hid.

THE HOME PRESENTED LIKE A PLACE FORBIDDEN. Worn-down steps, weathered walls, thick imposing double doors stranded behind a tarnished gate. By a miracle of engineering, the doors and gate, heavy as they are, open almost effortlessly, exposing a well-staged entry façade that leads to a row of offices, one by one down a cavernous hall. Globe lights hang from chromium pipes, each outside a windowed door that spells-out what goes on in there. STAFF, FINANCE, PERSONNEL. None say what they do for the kids.

Beneath a sign—SIGN-IN HERE—I gave a name, and a voice came back. *One floor up. Two-one-two. Left side, past the attendants' station.*

Michael was alone, shirt unbuttoned, belly exposed, rocking in a wicker rocking chair, a whiff of something when he rocked back, but masked somewhat when he returned. They'd cut his hair off pretty much—a "baldy sour," we said as kids—exposing the shape of a trapezoid, suggesting to me, for the first time really, that something's missing, not something's wrong. His pants—someone else's pants?—seemed to me too short too, the cuffs set high over scruffy shoes, the crotch soiled in a days-old way. He looked like someone else to me, someone I've seen but can't quite place. Then the face came through to me. The face of Kay's absent father in the photos she hadn't clipped him from.

Leaning in, I spoke to Michael but knew that there was no one there. Facing forward—quiet, stiff—he stared straight down at something on the floor but not at anything I could see. He was in the room and not in the room, reminding me of my grandmother, years ago in nursing care, her mind given over to, *Senility,* we said—then said, *Dementia,* years later when my aging mother took her place.

Sitting on the bed, talking to him, I looked in close at crust on his lids and then in the mirror facing me—at broken lines on my weathered face, arranged in the shape of matching brackets; at dashes around blood-shot eyes made smaller under bloated lids; at cuts on my cheek aside my nose forming the slope of misplaced commas.

Do signs that speak to a person's past punctuate their face?

UNLIKE OTHERS IN OUR MIDDLE SCHOOL, Kay went on to a private high school, months after girls in our eighth-grade class fingered her as the last of them to have had her first period. Teens are tough to hide things from, like a boy in school we all called "Pipes" after he had his colon fixed.

Us kids were all from church-going families, but Kay's was altogether different. Her mother, for one, was all in. Hands on a Bible, when not in the sink, pleading her case for life after death; on high alert for a non-believer or anyone living in a secular way. Pick a topic, any topic—raising kids, a movie, a book—and she'd let you know what the church would say. All by herself, Kay's mother was our first clue that whatever a mother's role is, part of the role is to be a pest.

We all liked Kay, everyone did, but her moving on to another school landed like a relief to us, since her mother was getting in everyone's way. We were teens—we all were— with no interest in biblical guidance or in doing a church's bidding on earth. We weren't bad kids. We were curious, adventurous, healthy kids—just like kids were anywhere, even the ones, Kay's mother said, *With the gall to think, God forbid, that Heaven would welcome a non-believer.*

I do think much less harshly now. Just saying what we all thought then.

I didn't lay eyes on Kay for a while, not till sometime after high school, leaving a bar that allowed us in. I looked up, saw her walking alone, and made the conversion frame by frame like a slow-motion camera from the girl I remembered to the woman I saw. Her walk was mature, head held high, and her well exercised, grownup body was carefully calibrated into place. She looked good. Quite good.

Looking away, I walked away. No use reaching over my head.

Well, well, I heard Kay say, then heard her mumble something else, maybe even my first name. She recognized me—and that alone I took as good, since girls who look as good as her don't often turn my way. Hands in my pockets, I walked toward her.

She worked in a costume-jewelry shop, linking stones to chokers and chains, biding time till her boat came in. In the fall, she'd enrolled in a junior college to train for something, *More like a calling than just a job.*

A calling?

What's wrong with a job to make ends meet? Seemed like a lot of crap to me but I went along, just the same.

Social work?

No, no. Accounting, she said, glancing back to the entry door. Accounting?

Books? I asked.

I could be a CPA.

I told her I had some hours in English—to which she said what everyone did, *To get into what?* she said.

We didn't get much further than that—idle updates on kids we knew, reminders of the dumb things we all did, vague intentions for the numbers we exchanged—but further than if I'd walked away. We made no plans, nothing like that. Just claims to cross paths soon again, although not on the grounds of a college campus, given she said—I think in jest—that, *Accountants don't mix with English majors!*

That was the last thing either of us said.

I DIDN'T SEE KAY OR HEAR FROM HER until what seems a year later. My heartrate quickened and my breathing stalled when KAY appeared on my cell. Kay? A butt dial? Let it ring? I was too anxious to let it ring.

She was on her back in a hospital bed. *The off-ramp by the fire station. Three other cars, two totaled,* she said. *Not my fault,* she thought to say. She'd been in the hospital alone for days.

Bump into someone you knew as a kid and then, maybe a year later, they call you from a hospital bed? I did my best to hold my end of a call I wasn't prepared for.

Stop by today? I'll tell you more.

Sure, I said. Blurted, really. *Should be there in an hour or so.*

Okay, she said. *Talk soon.*

I drove to the hospital preoccupied—why'd she call, to what end?—but aware of the sound of the pouring rain, delivery trucks, screeching brakes; all of them pounding in my head. I was sure of myself in the parking lot. Confident, I guess you'd say, my headache notwithstanding. *She* called me and *she* invited me to visit. This can't be bad and could be good. But walking up the hospital steps, my heartrate quickened more than before. Worse than that, my hairline dampened like it often did when I was nervous or down-right scared. I calmed myself as best I could—sips of water, washing my face—and entered her room anyway.

Her arm was broken and her legs banged-up in a way that crimped the flow of blood, leaving a limp and recurring pain she'd live with going forward. But even laid up in a hospital bed—no makeup, prone, a faded johnny—she looked as good as she ever did. We talked for a while, quite a while. Back and forth, like we had outside the bar that night, though this time seemed different. This time she took to looking at me, rather than away or over my shoulder—to what she might be missing.

There was no one else to call, she said and, owing to constant pious rants, preferred to keep her mother away. "No one else" was honest, I guess, but not what I hoped that she would say. And not for her mother to say months later that unless we marry in a church she approves—and before a priest she questioned first—God would condemn us both on earth. I don't know why Kay married me or even why I asked, except that at a certain age it's what you do with who's in range. And judging from her saying "no one else," neither of us had someone in range.

Kay's pregnancy brought some potent scares: cysts, fatigue, and a thyroid problem that explained the weight she piled on and the spotting that sent her straight to bed. She carried on with little fuss, humbling me to realize that mothers almost everywhere do things children never see—and if they saw, would soon forget.

Nine out of ten on the Apgar, Kay said, a newborn body nestled in her arms, the browns of his eyes bright and knowing. All we saw was clement weather. A brand-new baby, a place to live, and the gift of an absent mother-in-law, who claimed she'd never welcome the child of a marriage sealed by a Justice of the Peace.

If I had to say, and I often have, I'd say that a woman out of my league settled for a man with little to offer, other than the will to endure the role of a man who'd married above his head. Little to offer—and little to say when a change toward me came over Kay that, thinking back, made some sense, given that, in our case, fate was a crash by a fire station.

KAY WAS AWAKE WHEN I GOT BACK from a job an hour away. Most of my jobs the past few months were little more than day labor, since hiring bosses wouldn't know that I was prone to arrive late when Kay ignored her meds. Late and I'd miss the morning lineup, but bosses wouldn't know a thing. If I'm not there, they don't care since there'd be others to take my place.

Me being away meant Kay was alone, which meant she had some time to brood and might have something blunt to say.

She did. *A man supports you. You let him,* she said. *You make a life with the kids,* she said. She stepped toward me then turned away.

What do you say to a thing like that? *What do you want from me, Kay?*

She turned. *A lot of things, I want,* she said, *like a kid that walks and claps his hands—that no one had to take away!*

I say she "said" but she was screaming.

You married me for what? I asked.

No one marries for a reason why. You marry when it's time— to what's there then. On that, I guess, we thought the same.

We didn't talk in the coming days or the day she felt the time had come to go by bus to visit Michael. I found her there when I walked in, unconsciously chewing her bottom lip, leaning forward in a straight-back chair, eyes directed toward Michael, who stared ahead like he often did, this time at a low watt bulb that kept the coming dark at bay. There she was and there she wasn't. Conscious I thought, though I couldn't say, except that both her eyes were open, the light bulb lurking beside her head.

She looked to me like the walking dead, the body double of making do.

I PICKED UP MICHAEL FOR A BIRTHDAY, his, and just for the afternoon. I hoped for a sunny, blue-sky day, not for dark gray clouds and rain. Not for Michael's first trip home. *See he eats,* an attendant said, under an open golf umbrella he held above our heads. Truth is, I had a funny feeling—a gnawing, empty, grim feeling—bringing Michael home for the day. A lie would be that I wanted to, not knowing for sure what Kay would do.

Michael lost all sign of calm—furrowed brow, grinding teeth—as we drove by places he would have known in earlier days. Lido's Beach, where he'd wade for hours at water's edge; Crescent Park, where he'd board a train in Peanut Land, a kiddy-ride beneath his age. Calm returned with the sound of tires on the bed of stones beside our place. I released the buckle that held him in and let him push my hand away. He often pushed my hand away—not in anger, the attendant said, more as a sign of independence that had nothing to do with me.

Kay appeared, fully dressed, from her now near-constant bedroom exile. She'd decorated as best she could—a "Happy Birthday" tablecloth, chocolate frosted birthday cake, and two standing number candles that added up to about his age. Michael stomped on the outdoor mat, then scraped his muddy overshoes on a tattered indoor throw. I stood on the step directly behind him, alert if he should wobble back but careful not to let him know.

Shut the door! Kay said to me in a tone that seemed to pierce the air. *The door!* she said again.

Startled by her voice or something else, Michael's body stiffened straight. There was something in the way he looked at her. And the way she looked at him.

Looking down, he lunged ahead two full steps, and impounded all his weight and fury into a backward flying fist that contorted Kay's mouth and cheeks, like a close-up shot of a half-dazed fighter stunned by a punch that landed square. He seemed possessed—fully possessed—in a frightful glee at the intersect of relieving a hard-to-reach itch and claiming sweet revenge.

DON'T QUITE KNOW WHAT COMES OF THIS, the home's director said to me, before he said, in his opinion, *Michael can't be released to you if Kay decides to press charges,* for what she says that I did to land her in a hospital bed.

Press charges? What *I* did?

He looked at me with an arrogant grin that served to confirm his hold on me. This would be my worst day yet.

Turned away from Michael and Kay, I rose from a chair set lower than his and left without a word, oddly content in a newfound freedom walking away endowed in me. *Who needs this?* I thought to myself, until I walked alone outside. Exiled, ousted, and estranged—but a child I still had hope for.

A month later, maybe more, the sum of my things is packed in boxes stacked in a hall by a room I rent. *Move 'em,* the landlord says again and likely said to others before with hardly a hint of opposition from tongues beat back on hardened people who don't talk back, even in the face of more on the way, much like more's in store for me. I stand in the hall outside my room and struggle with a box too wide to lift, my mind drifting from Kay to Michael—one caged for now, the other for good—and then to me, alone now with the things I'm scared of—including Kay's revenge.

II.

An Absence of Speech

Will you? she asks with what she can spare from a tongue parched white by the toxin she's fed. A maze of collaborating tubes and bags huddle together on a rack by her bed—upright, tall, immobile, mute—a vertical sentry remanding her body to a state she wouldn't be spared from.

She's still who she was when I was a child. Tranced in thought, fingers on beads, committed deeply to the power of prayer that somehow seemed subservient to me. "Blessed art thou"? "Hallowed be thy name"? She appeared to know too much of a God, who had good reason to hold things close. But she knew enough—she was good that way—to treat my youthful dissent with grace. How did I come to pray here now, years removed from my younger days, reciting in silence prayers she taught me to say as a child, kneeling beside my big girl bed and then, still a teen, to repeat to myself?

My tongue touches folds on the roof of my mouth, an O drags air from my trembling throat. *No,* I say—although not to her face—to veins on hands that comforted me, our places reversed, her in a vigil beside my bed and me in traction from a swimming pool prank that, despite days of discouraging news, failed to disable me permanently.

I can't, I say in reply to the words her lips turn rigid from forming.

Her eyes are weepy from what I said—or from what she's struggling to ask of me.

Again, the repeating drip-drip-drip from an otherwise silent IV bag, making it clear, at least to me, that all there is now is the slimmest of margins and all there was then was the odds of things.

Why? she says, until she catches herself.

Why not? she whispers soon thereafter, a shooting pain having returned her, if only for now, to the courage she showed before I was born, redeeming herself for sins she committed when little more than a child herself. Pregnant at far too early an age, she dismissed the appeal of public assistance and resisted pleas to "give it away," a minister said, and "be done with it," her grandmother said.

In and out, the resident says. *Consciousness,* I hear him say.

And he's right. I've seen that throughout the night—and seen an alternating back and forth in her state of mind and in her reaction to a host of things. Fear, then courage; pain, then relief; disbelief in the face of decline, then faith that the end has beginnings to bring.

Is she today, facing this day, fraught with the anguish that trapped her before, faced with the choice of delivering me—of keeping me?

Reaching to arrange the pillow by her head, I hear her say what I didn't see coming.

Alive, she says, *means … wanting … to be,* gasping and coughing at "means" and "to be," her whole body bent into what she is saying.

Who among us doesn't hang by a thread above what we think is the reason to pray? And what is that thread but the dark of night? I don't tell her that. I say instead, *I want you to be.*

Need you to be, I should have said.

Her speech recedes to a breathy whisper. And her face and her eyes show me, I see, that I am not who she wants me to be. Show me I'm not who I ought to be. I am failing her—and in ways that she didn't fail me.

There is in the air an absence of speech.

There is in each of her distant eyes a fully translucent, glossy film. She can focus, I think, or want to think, but the arc of pain is piercing, cutting.

Between us, now, there is gesture only. Blinking, pointing, a head nod, a wink.

She retreats to a place inside of herself, far removed now from awkward pleas, pinned in place by a catheter, pain, a blanket, and faith.

I lean in to look. To look closer at her.

No! I say with all there is that's in me to say it—and in a way I've never said anything before.

Standing Perfectly Still
on the Table

A lightbulb shines on bolts of fabric in a kitchen that doubles as a sewing room. Determined, a young boy surveys the room, searching for a pattern and a wooden ruler. The pattern, somewhere here on the table, is fastened, he thinks, with a safety pin from a basket the last man brought for the mother after she started seeing him. The man before—the second man?—had a kind, welcoming way, different from the last man's cynical ways. He took at once to smiling at the mother, smiling at the boy, never once raising his voice to them. That was nice, the boy told his mother—the smiling was, the calm voice was—but not until the second man left fed-up and the last man started appearing more, reawakening the sensitive boy to the second man's peaceful ways.

The boy knew better than to tell his mother that her smile had faded, and her voice seemed tentative, softer, weak.

The first man, a young man—too young, maybe—abandoned the ever-resourceful mother, who long since developed a way with fabric, relying on remnants, instinct, and patterns to fashion for herself, for others, or the boy—clothes she'd assemble at the kitchen table, measured to spec with a yardstick or a ruler, early gifts the first man brought well before his patience gave. Sewing to the boy was an outsized joy, since the mother had begun to rely on him more, particularly on those accumulating days when she seemed to the boy gloomy, low. She had taken to calling him a trusted apprentice. "Trusted" the boy had heard before, but "apprentice" was a new word to him, a word that only a grownup would say, a word that made him feel good.

Tell you what, she says to the boy, who perks up to hear what his mother will say.

Let's do like they do in a tailor shop.

Like they do, like what? the young boy says.

This ruler, here, stood on end, makes a hemline guide for a longer dress, like the one we're making now.

The boy wasn't sure what his mother was saying.

I'll stand on the table, the mother says. *You pin the hemline, sitting at the table!*

Why don't I kneel on the floor? he asks.

This puts the hem at eye level.

The boy's face gleams.

I turn, you pin, she says to the boy. *I turn, you pin,* she says again. *Place the pins a little bit apart. This much,* she says, holding her thumb and forefinger up. She pulls out a chair from the kitchen table, climbs on the chair to the tabletop, and motions the boy to sit in the chair. *Gorgeous, the dress you and I will make, like you've heard some of my clients say.*

The boy interrupts to correct his mother. *Our clients!* the young boy says, proud that he got what "client" meant—just like he got what "apprentice" meant, without even having to ask.

Standing perfectly still on the table, bedazzled in a gown of brocade fabric sewn with only a temporary hem from the pattern the young boy found on the table, she shimmies into the top of the dress—the bodice, she teaches the boy to say—and tells the boy, who's sitting at the table, *Stick on the gown, at the 10s, a pin. Ten inches up, at the 10,* she says.

A pin, she says. *Straight up, perfectly straight, the ruler,* she says to the timid but helpful boy to whom she's been both mother and father.

The boy hasn't met his biological father, and the mother doesn't mention the long-gone man. The boy doesn't mention his father either. The young boy knows, or has come to know, that his father is best unspoken of. He certainly knows, somehow knows, that as time goes by, but not just yet, he could ask his mother where his father went and, more to the point, what he doesn't get. A parade of men bound to move in—some nice, most not, like the men with them—why wouldn't a father live with his kids? Most fathers do, don't they?

Turn, the boy says to the mother, both of his hands released from the fabric, and she does—one step—on the kitchen table. Then, *Stop!* the boy shouts to the mother, after her two feet come to a rest. She does, she freezes, and he does too, waiting for the sway of the hem to still, waiting to place another of the pins at exactly the height where the last one is.

They were doing well, she told him so, her standing tall, him cautious with the pins. And they will again on another day, if not for hers, then another woman's dress, like the one they're sewing for a mother-of-the-bride, enabling them to afford what they need. Sewing supplies, bolts of fabric, rent, utilities, food for the table, and the cellphone she bought to replace the one the boy heard crash on the bedroom wall, but she said merely fell on the floor.

Atop the table at a dizzying height, she scans the kitchen, the walls, the floor, noticing things she'd seen before but now from an angle new to her. A window valence fraying at the seams, the ceiling stained from cooking oil, the unfinished top of a pantry door. But oddly, given the length of his stay, nothing in the room remains of the first man—the longest to stick around, by far—not even the wall marks she repaired, except for the ruler and the metal yardstick she struggles at night to uncouple him from. And she struggles, too, independent of him—more now than before, she's come to admit—when the knot in her belly feels heavy, taut, her thin body stiffened from an empty void a brochure led her to think she's in.

From here on the table, turning her head, she can see in the bedroom to her unmade bed where, huddled in a quilt—groggy, fatigued but short of the restful sleep she needs—she lies awake and succumbs most nights to a dreamful urge. To assume the form of a bird on the wing, taking to flight at the moment of flight, relying on instinct, reflex, whim, to soar at will, to glide unencumbered, to disembody from the weight of herself, an escape from the suffocating tunnel she's in. There's a way, she knows, to disembody but she also knows—the first man taught her—that the trouble with drugs is they work at first.

I'm glad we'll be alone, the boy says, returning her to the task at hand and startling her to realize that, without her having said a word, the young boy senses that the last man will be leaving soon, gone with his indifference intact, just like the men before him did. *I'm glad,* he says again to his mother, who reaches into her jeans back pocket through an unsown seam on the side of the dress.

One more pin, one more, he says, both hands raised from the task at the table.

That's quite enough ..., begins the mother, glancing at the hem now circled in pins.

She holds in one hand the brand-new phone and positions with the other the overhead bulb. *... of this,* the mother says to herself, a hushed but ever so powerful call to alter the fabric of lives played out at a kitchen table. Phone held high, she aims the camera toward the smiling boy, the first man to seem to understand that this time, again—like every other time—she'll emerge from the tunnel whole again, ushered by the boy who'll become a man.

Both hands holding the hem aloft, she carefully steps from the table to the chair to the kitchen floor, then turns the chair to face the boy. It's cumbersome moving in a pinned-up dress but she feels the urge to speak to the boy in a way she hopes more tactile than speech. Sitting together, face to face, she leans in slightly, smiles at him, places her hands on the young boy's face, and files his cheeks with her fingerprints—a gesture he'll use when the time comes later for another man to raise his kids.

Done at Thirty

Driving away in a rental car, the daughter leaves her parents' house after letting her father know what her mother knew already.

She's kidding, the father says to the mother. *He's done this how many times before?*

She'll be the third, the mother says.

And she's okay with done at thirty? he asks.

Right, she says. *She thought it through. It's what she wants.*

That's outrageous! How can you just sit there? Our daughter! he says. *What kind of crap is that, this guy!*

You think it's better she didn't know?

He doesn't have an answer for that. He's on his feet and pacing. *I can't believe it,* the father says. *You actually support her in this?*

Not at first, the mother says.

Why? he says.

It's what she wants. Twenty-two. She makes her own decisions. She is slouching back in a bentwood chair, sipping from a coffee cup.

How old is he, this horse's ass? the father asks. *Thinks these women are lining up.*

They have lined up, the mother says.

He has an answer for that. *Then she's the horse's ass!* he says. *Your daughter! How old's this guy, I asked you.*

Forty two, I think, she says.

The father walks to the mother's chair. *Eight years, he'll be fifty!*

Yes, that's right, she says to him. *And what's she want with him after that?*

Carp

Fitting a float arm into place, my mother turned from the bowl toward me to whisper another of the truths we knew. *Even before his shift, he smelled.* I rushed a glance at my mother's eyes, turned from the bathroom toward the hall, and walked to my father's idling car—him in the front, gear in the trunk, and me in the back to listen.

Not to talk, to listen.

Fish for the week. Jesus jumpin', don't do this. Make good, he said, often said, but clammed-up cold at the river's edge because, he said, *Carp know.* For a time, for weeks, I watched him close, learning to bait, to hook, to cast. I figured that when the time was right—another week, another month— he'd let me fish as well. In time, in months, I came to know I'd never cast a line with him. He couldn't afford a second pole. Or couldn't afford to let me fool with the tools he used to feed himself.

I kept quiet, except to my mother, who knew I wouldn't call him out. Knew without a word from me.

Withdrawn in an era when no one noticed, he'd given up, my mother said, resigned to years on an overnight shift maintaining presses in a stamping plant that left most workers hard of hearing from an endless, high pitched, punch and clang in ears that few protected. He didn't seem to notice the noise. And why would he, I suppose, given the blasts—really, the damning, ear ringing blasts—he said he'd heard from M1 rifles fired in Europe in World War II and Browning automatic M1918s platoons carried in the soon to follow Korean War he bravely re-enlisted for?

Why both wars? I thought to myself, though not till the romance of foreign war had faded away with childhood.

I asked my mother.

She didn't know.

HILL-AND-DALE, I SAID AS A KID—whatever I thought a "dale" was—driving the rolling countryside, sitting in the back of our pickup truck, swaying around and over myself, while my mother drove erratically. *Get ready!* she'd yell on an empty road, then drive like hell until I had enough. And some days I had more than enough, near throwing up in a cargo bed my mother polished to a flawless glow.

That's enough! I'd scream to her, but she could tell if it really was. If it was, she'd stop. If it wasn't, *No!* I called it a game of cat and mouse. She called it a game of chicken, she'd say, with the little boy who cried wolf.

She was all the fun back then. She cooked with pride, fed me good, and let me skip Sunday school if I took to pleading enough with her. And the one who would stand up for me with teachers, proprietors, neighbors, cops. No one messed with my mother, I tell you. My father was the complacent one. A soldier but the complacent one. Who would have guessed it would be that way?

WHY DOESN'T TIME DULL THE IMAGE of seeing her run—my mother run—from our lean-to garage to the kitchen door, arms surrounding a bowling bag, disheveled like the teacher in my homeroom, who told my mother in a note to home that my school clothes reeked of whatever my parents were doing at home?

Reeked, my mother read out loud. *Doing at home,* she said out loud, not saying what else the teacher wrote.

I knew not to swear in my mother's presence but, not unlike an ill-timed sneeze, I let out, *Bastard,* anyway.

Are you kidding me? my mother said but I think she meant the teacher.

Who, for God's sake, has the right—what middle school teacher has the right, wearing that same damn sweater daily—to tread toward judgment on a student's home, particularly a home that housed a veteran of foreign wars? Two foreign wars! He could be a hero, for all she knows. Doesn't that count for just enough to keep her damned mouth shut?

Being the man of the house now—a stretch, but that's what my mother said—I took the liberty, for the first time ever, to affix blame to my absent father and tell my mother what I thought of him, more harshly maybe than a grown man would in a barrage of thoughts that didn't quit. *Never talked to either of us, not even at the kitchen table, staring ahead at whatever was there—a butter dish, a carton of milk. The stench of stale tobacco on him, the gall to leave the toilet broke.* And that wasn't all I thought of him.

My mother could tell I was piling on, but that's not what she said. She defended him instead. *He worked steady, living here. Came straight home from work,* she said, a generous spin on the life he led.

Punched out at seven in the morning! I said. *Where would he go, that time of day, other than come straight home?*

That seemed to get her, what I said. She sighed, inhaled, and turned toward me, one brow raised above the other, eyes as bright as the scales on a carp. *Your father,* she said, *has never been out of the States,* she said.

What Scrimshaw Leaves Unsaid

If only the rain hadn't fallen together, provoking the coast-line to float face down, muting the call of a bar-tailed godwit—stranded, fragile, wing in hand. Rising from the marsh, the call falls flat on a seabed immobile below a tide driven by a thrashing ocean wind that carried the godwit, battered and torn. If somehow the saltmarsh could heal the bird, stranded in a trance that other birds know, wading in a stand of coastal reed—groping, limping, beak down to forage for no reason other than habit calls.

If godwits in number should gather in the marsh, would any be able to rescue the bird or even have reason to commune with a bird going the natural way of birds? Each would know, having seen this before, the fate of a wing gone tragically awry and the futility of fending for an injured bird, rather than attend to the sustenance in reach, the cover in sight, and the respite before an arduous journey their thin wings have yet to travel.

Completing a year after year migration leaves so little life to spend in vain, so little time for a battered bird but more than enough accumulated wisdom, gathered through trial or evolution, to grasp in ways humans wouldn't the potent insult a whaler unleashes, even if unwittingly, in scrimshaw the whaler carves in bone that illegal whaling would leave behind. Scrimshaw spares bones from willful waste but the godwit sees what a whaler wouldn't. The tearing apart of flesh and bone releases the dead whale's foregone soul.

What a whaler needs for scrimshaw is a knife and a whale and a lie to tell in lyric or verse through a veil of ink in interlocking lines that leverages the whaler's well-honed skills to lure a collector's yearning for enchantment, claiming in lines the splendor of the sea by no means other than slices and cuts that offend the godwit's reverence for the whale, incarnate with others perished in vain, and exacerbate the godwit's loathing for the whaler, a super-empowered weather-worn rogue, brought to the shore like the stranded bird, upending the natural evolution of a species, living the God forsaken life only an itinerant whaler would, aware of laws that outlaw their work but ignorant of the godwit's awareness of them.

How much we miss—I certainly miss—absent the savvy to interpret signs wholly abundant in our oncoming path, registering nothing in the lax among us, save for what we stumble upon. In the ebbing tide, I happen to notice the leftover remnants of a well-worn bone, the color various shades of gray; the edges smooth from saltwater, beach sand, weathering wind. And happen to notice in a shallow dune the gray-blue, brick-red injured godwit stranded in the weight of a broken wing, walking slowly to go unnoticed, then scurrying franticly when I step near.

The bone in my hand, the godwit in view, I turn toward the sea, the oddly quiet and windless sea—one day before, a raging sea—and imagine the collection of ships that have passed, a vast armada over hundreds of years, steaming, sailing, rowing, floating, in overlapping lines of simulated travel, visible in the unobstructed view of generations of birds in flight, including the godwit moored in the marsh, unable it seems to continue to travel but consumed in my presence in a high-pitched chatter with little other than me in view.

I stand and linger in the calm around me, close both eyes, raise both hands, and imagine the power to lift the coastline, the marsh, the reed to witness signs that the godwit saw in flight overhead, migrating from Alaska's inland brush to the northern edge of Australia's shore—fragments of shipwrecks, fossil remains, baleen, teeth, rotting flesh—and saw aloft, contemporaneously, whalers carving bone into shape and saw what birds have repeatedly seen, more even than the whaler sees and certainly more than I could see—how the telltale lines on scrimshaw are read from a seasoned godwit's point of view.

The godwit belies what the scrimshaw claims in a song that trembles in furious conviction, insisting in vain that the whaler confess what the scrimshaw reveals was done at will, likely at dusk and far enough at sea to mask the slaughter of a life-giving whale that could only be felt in an animate way if the line art is read by a knowing bird, aghast at the carnage adrift near shore, disabled by a wing gone limp in the wind but anxious to interpret for collectors to hear the anguish in a slaughtered whale's voice that pirated scrimshaw leaves unsaid.

A Daughter's Conviction

*The female weavers assembled to the number of one hundred
and two. The result was a resolution to abandon their looms.*

—*Manufacturers and Farmers Journal*
Providence, Rhode Island, May 31, 1824

No less sudden than a shooting star, she rose, this daughter of a fate foretold, young but nameless in the records
that survive, including the diaries of weaving-mill barons—
each an owner of a breathtaking mansion none of the mill
weavers dared tread near—to lead one hundred and one
other women, bleeding from wear to fingers and hands, the
first in history to rise together in a walk-off-the-shop-floor
labor strike, absent men too timid at first to turn from their
mechanized weaving looms to the exits of wood-frame textile mills in defiance of the town's merchant barons, who'd
ordered a twenty percent cut in wages and one hour more
to a long workday.

Who were *you*, who took the reins? Daughters of the
mothers of the Revolution, mothers of the daughters who'd
turn suffragettes, the models I told my daughter about to
re-enact in a grade-school sketch—Susan B. Anthony, Ida
B. Wells—before she explored deeper on her own, before
she discovered the textile weavers who, to this day, remain

unnamed but have everything to do with my daughter's conviction to join in union with like-minded sisters, traveling by foot on foreign soil to care for the children of ailing parents too feeble to care for the children themselves.

I told her this when she was young. Years later, she told me more. *The ones unnamed, unknown,* she said. *The ones in the mills two centuries ago. The Sisters, _my_ sisters, with the children now.* The ones I came to know about, if only by the words my daughter spoke, spoken in letters she wrote to me, nights from makeshift triage stations, exhausted from nursing unfed children, their welfare unstable in fractured homes, if not for the balance my daughter brought.

These are the daughters our daughters should know.

Inside the Jewelry Store Window

I *can't,* I said. *Please,* I said. *I can't,* I said to what he said to do. *Take it,* he said.

No, I said.

It's yours, he said.

No, I said back.

He stomped the floor with the heel of his boot. *This is your chance to get it,* he said.

Reaching over the glass counter, he pulled the velvet curtain back. *Take it,* he said. *Reach in!*

I reached, I did—I tell you I did—but knew I couldn't in quite the way I can when no one's looking.

I can't, I said.

Jesus, he said. *Who do you know don't take what's theirs?* He dropped the curtain, picked up my face, and looked in my eyes, up close and in.

I can't, I said.

It's yours! he said.

I gotta pee.

They looked at each other, then looked at me.

Pee? he asked.

At a robbery? his girlfriend said.

Ain't robbery, he said.

I gotta, I do! I said.

Time like this, you pee? he said.

Let the poor kid pee, she said.

What the hell you talkin'? he said. *Kids got iron bladders, for Christ's sake. Every kid, a bladder like that.*

Takes after you, she said to him.

I started to walk.

Where you goin'?

To pee, I said.

He turned, sighed, and scratched his head.

I walked away from the two of them, over to where the toilet was—behind a counter, down a hall, and through a far too squeaky door. And maybe away from the whole damn thing. What would my mother think of me, doing this in here with them? On a "precipice" is where I was, the very first time in my life till then—maybe in my life after then!—that a blasted middle school vocabulary word would be the word that worked.

I flushed the toilet, washed my hands, stood in place as long as I could, and walked to where the two of them were, standing aside the counter and curtain.

What the hell were you doin'? he said.

Easy, she said.

You ready? he said.

No, I said.

I let you pee! he said, louder than he should.

Keep your damn voice down, she said.

Look, I got this figured, he said to her.

She looked at him.

Reach in, take it, he said to me. *As much as you can.* He held the velvet curtain back. *Reach!*

I leaned this time. I reached. I did.

You got this figured? she said to him.

Yeah, he said.

You? she said.

He didn't answer.

You wouldn't be here, it weren't for me.

Kid's got it comin', he said to her.

The kid? she said, hands on her hips, looking straight at him.

He let the curtain fall from his hand. He turned to direct his attention to her. He couldn't have been more focused on her. Not in my mother's store, he couldn't.

Is This a Good Time?

Carolyn's gait was so graceful and poised that her movement, almost anywhere in the room, tilted the center of gravity with her. More imposing, to Peter at least, was the uncommon insight in comments she made, some brimming with nuance and wit he rarely witnessed in non-degree students.

How might a win be a loss at trial? Peter asked.

Well, she answered when no one did, *if the court awards a small-dollar judgment, you can't appeal a case you won!* He continued to speak—to lecture, really—eyes straight ahead, both hands aloft, his mind's eye focused on a sharp reply that avoided the lure of fussy jargon.

Peter was a powerful speaker and desperately shy, a self-proclaimed activist and an infrequent champion of activist causes, a contradictory man who, by teaching continuing legal education courses—Appellate Updates, Motion Practice—was able to accommodate clubs and vacations beyond the reach of his university salary. But Carolyn didn't see contradiction. Like others in the course, she saw instead a sensitive man who'd worried visibly about a breakroom attendant who'd taken ill suddenly. He seemed to possess an authentic vulnerability not unlike, as one student put it, John Cazale's roles the decade before. Sal, say, in *Dog Day Afternoon* or Fredo in *The Godfather.*

An administrative matter, Peter said, sweat beads forming below his hairline. *Cabs and trains being what they are, is anyone driving by O'Hare by chance?* She raised her hand—and from what he could tell, without hesitation. But so had a balding, middle-aged man with a patently dramatic—annoying?—habit of punctuating his high-pitched speech with stagey arm-waving arabesques of emphasis, disarming to anyone with a glass in their hand.

Thanks, Carolyn, Peter said.

In the car, he saw her from a different angle—from the side, up close, unobstructed—a view that exposed a scar by her brow, maybe the remains of chicken pox or maybe a childhood accident. Hands on the wheel, looking ahead, Carolyn appeared decidedly composed, a self-assured woman who wasn't even the least bit unsettled by the sidewise glances of a man who, apart from his insights on federal appeals, was little more than a stranger to her. As they spoke, he stared at the rings on her fingers, the pendant on her neck, and the shape of the buckles on her Birkenstock shoes, exposed fully by a rising hem as she worked the pedals of the accelerator and brake. But their time in the car was slipping away, threatening Peter's only chance to channel the conversation from polite chit-chat to the forward but guarded invitation that could very well lead to defeat.

Carolyn lowered the radio's volume and adjusted the visor to shelter her eyes.

Maybe I should bring the quiet ones out. Get 'em involved, he said.

Could be the material, Carolyn said. *Most are there for the hours, the CLE credit. Few, I'm guessing, file appeals.*

Peter didn't want the conversation to lag. But he needed a pause, time to gather the nerve to say something—anything that would prevent their brief alliance from ending abruptly curbside. He lingered a bit, then went all in. *Carolyn, my wife may come … come back when I'm back for a course in September. Think you might like to join us for dinner? Your husband, too.*

I'd like that, Carolyn said. *You don't have class?*

Law school's after the undergrads. Late September this year.

There was silence now, save for jet exhausts off in the distance and a song on the radio that Carolyn lip-synced and Peter didn't know. As the "Departures" sign appeared overhead, Carolyn pulled the car to the curb. They did not speak—save for "thanks" from Peter, "glad to" from her, and "I'll write when I know" from him. Peter cradled his bag in his arms, stepped to the sidewalk, and closed the passenger door behind him. He didn't turn to make eye contact with her and neither did she with him.

THE NOTE PETER MAILED IN EARLY September gave every sign of having been composed. He made the predicable excuse for his wife—"Two extra days on Cape Cod seemed more inviting to Laura than two on Chicago's concrete!"—and, in closing, he shifted the burden to Carolyn. "I'll be at the Drake on Walton. Arrive Sunday about five p.m.; depart Tuesday a.m. Leave a message at the front desk. Or call." Innocent enough. The last line, though—"(Sure looking forward to seeing you)"—was risky. Not for the encouragement but for the parentheses. They seemed to invoke an intimacy, as if he had whispered the words to her.

Three weeks later he returned through O'Hare.

A message for me? Peter asked the desk clerk, whose head was down in search of a room.

No, sir.

You're sure? T-I.

Sir?

Ends in T-I, Peter said. *C-O-R-R-E-N-T-I not T-E. Thought maybe you might have misspelled.*

No, sir. There's no message. Turning his head, raising his voice, the desk clerk called, *Front!*

Entering the street view room with a bellman, Peter glanced at the room phone message light on the off chance the desk clerk had been mistaken. The light was off, even on close inspection.

Although weary from the flight and the train to the Loop, Peter remained dressed, mostly—in case she called from the lobby or hall—and passed the time staring at a TV station that signed off minutes after Ralph and Alice embraced in a *Honeymooners* rerun. He changed, went to bed, slept restlessly, and woke in a sweat-filled frenzy. What if she didn't call? And what if she hadn't gotten his note?

Preoccupied, Peter was less than impressive in class, a fitting prelude as he walked north on Michigan Avenue, back to the Drake at the end of the day. He paused in the near-empty hotel lobby, stepped from the elevator hurriedly, then proceeded hopefully to his room. The unlit telephone message light—a cold, blackened red—dimmed what remained of his dwindling hope.

But what was the point of worrying? So what if she hadn't received his note or, worse, had simply ignored it? It wasn't as if their conversation in the car was binding. Besides, he didn't want to betray Laura, or even be inconsiderate of her, although Laura hardly mattered in this. What mattered was that Peter had reached a point where he wanted to live a more absorbing lifestyle. A daily routine subject to enviable last-minute change (*Professor Correnti, could you stay on this evening to meet some of the foundation's benefactors?*), a career that made him feel as though he were working out of deeper necessity than the word "career" implied (he was a popular classroom teacher and a solid producer of legal scholarship, but he wasn't a teacher's teacher or a scholar's scholar). No ifs, ands, or buts about it, Peter Correnti had invited new energy into his life in the form of Carolyn Cordova-Pitts, and he wasn't about to discourage it.

At exactly 6:17 p.m., the room phone rang.

Hello? he said, his voice hopeful.

Peter?

Yes.

It's Carolyn …

Carolyn! Hi!

Sorry I couldn't call earlier. Last night was hectic and today I had meetings. I just got out.

I just got in, myself. Peter's zeal overcame him. He had to know immediately. *So, you free?*

Sure.

Great. How 'bout meeting for a drink?

Okay, where? Carolyn said.

What's in the area? Peter asked.

Tell you what, I'm right next to the Hyatt Regency. Not the Park Hyatt at Water Tower. The Regency on Wacker. There's a lounge there on the second floor, I think it is, in the atrium. Take the escalator up and it's behind you, overlooking the river. The explicit directions gave Peter the comforting impression that, much like him, she was unwilling to leave their meeting to chance.

Peter walked south on Michigan toward the Hyatt, partly in anticipation and partly in the midst of a sobering thought. Where would the evening lead? Equally troubling, where did he *want* the evening to lead? He hadn't thought through either question. But then, he'd never before felt compelled to meet a woman privately, let alone in a lounge, soon before dark, when both time and opportunity are abundant. Oh, he'd been smitten before—obsessed, Laura said, though half kidding—by the bevy of wide-eyed female students who, year after year, were replaced again by like-aged students, most in their later twenties, if that. None that he'd approached with an ignoble pass but some to whom he'd gifted favored treatment—a break on a due date, an excused absence, the benefit of the doubt in a written submission. A mistake to take this next step with Carolyn? This inviting her out, this writing to her, this preoccupation with postal deliveries, this arranging an evening to meet with her? Well, the thought did occur to him passing through the Hyatt's revolving door entrance, suddenly feeling his pulse quicken and his hands turn cold, as if he'd stepped naked into an ice cold shower.

Carolyn stood on the second floor landing, saw him first, and approached from his rear as the escalator delivered him. He turned, their eyes met, and he made the conversion, frame by frame, like a slow motion camera, from the woman he remembered to the one here now. Her posture was erect, accented by artificially square shoulders that swayed in sequence with each forward stride, giving the impression of authority from a distance and dominance as she arrived. Her full black hair had been cut, exposing double pierced ears, a svelte neck, and a long, straight nose—a more regal look than he remembered. Her brown eyes seemed darker against near pure whites, but her makeup detracted, made heavier since summer by eyeliner added to her lower lids. And she was taller—higher heels? Even with these blemishes, she seemed to him out of his league.

Pleasantries exhausted, smiles in play, *Let's find a table,* Peter said. They walked toward a circular high-top table, his hand perched lightly on her lower back, as if he weren't certain where his hand should be, if it should be on her body at all. Mindful his hand may have gone too far—they'd shared, so far, so very few words—he didn't risk reaching to help with her coat or to pull out her chair. He'd work up to that when the time came later, if it did.

For over an hour, they talked nonstop. Sometimes in generalities—*The law's little more than a collection of rules designed to keep us from lying to each other*—and other times to draw a laugh—*Quick, look, isn't it funny how youthful hairdos have the opposite effect in middle age?* Neither one displayed conversational flaws—awkwardness or long pauses, say—although when she spoke, Carolyn seemed to find comfort looking anywhere other than into his eyes, which served well to suppress Peter's shyness. Good heavens, he reasoned, she's nervous with me?

I told Brian, 'What will I talk to this man about?' And I did invite him. But I knew he wouldn't come. She looked long enough to see Peter's reaction. And he did react.

It's fine he didn't, Peter said, testing to see if she'd recoil. She didn't. Courage in hand, he leaned in closer—a subtle turn toward familiarity she didn't seem unwilling to allow—then asked, *Grab a bite?*

Okay, what are you up for?

Anything, really, he said laughing, hands raised in indecision.

How 'bout drinks and hors d'oeuvres? she said. *There's a place in Bucktown not far from here.*

Sounds great, he said.

Peter reached to help with her coat, left a far too generous tip, and turned to scan whether nearby tables had been near enough to hear.

The cab ride was quick, the bar subdued and, as before, the conversation effortless.

Misdemeanor? You're kidding?

Right, Carolyn said. *Miss Demeaner! Spelled E-R. Fourth grade. Taught my mother, too.*

She probably didn't even realize.

Neither did I at that age! she said.

Apart from when he and Laura first dated, or occasionally in conversation with peers, Peter hadn't spoken so easily with a woman—an artifact of the drinks, he wondered, or the comfort they seemed to summon in each other? In fact, in the whole evening there was only one snag, if you could call it that.

Forty-two?!

You're surprised? Peter asked, knowing full well she was.

No, well yeah. It's just …. Well, I figured you're older from the examples in class. Like you misread Miranda when the decision came out. And adding up the years, they'd add up.

He'd not seen her flustered or nervous before—or the pink that began to build on her face. His instinct was to rescue her.

Well, plenty of celebrities date much younger people.

Right, Sinatra repeatedly, I think.

And I'm, what, a dozen years older?

About. Right.

And we're just having a drink! Peter said, partly in jest but mostly in defense.

Carolyn smiled, looked uncharacteristically into his eyes and said, *It's not that. It's that you look great.*

Peter felt gypped that the compliment arrived at the end of the evening, just moments before Carolyn would announce she'd be expected home soon. But he was getting ahead of himself. Why not gloat that she'd complimented him—a delayed reply to his having said, *It's fine he didn't.*

The ramp-up to comfort had come quickly for them but their streetside farewell was awkward, each of them seeming to realize that the life of the relationship would hinge entirely on what was said now.

Peter touched her shoulder lightly—not unlike a smitten boy. *Carolyn, I'll be back after Thanksgiving. I'm giving a talk. What do you say we get together?*

I'd love it, Carolyn said.

I'll write when I know more, he said.

Peter hailed two cabs in the street. Her back toward him, she entered her cab without a hitch. Backpedaling, Peter tripped on the curb, but not before her cab departed.

CAROLYN'S MARRIAGE WASN'T A BUST, but it did have challenges from the start. She'd married young to a financial planner in whose world upward mobility and the march toward retirement were the common ground for solidarity.

Brian rarely spoke to Carolyn about anything unrelated to his work (*career*, as he preferred to say) or to their modest though compounding investment portfolio (*the family jewels*). And owing to a congenital immune disorder, he slept incessantly—nine or ten hours many nights, despite mid-day or afternoon naps. If he sacrificed sleep, he'd risk contracting whatever ailment hovered around him—the flu, a cough, the common cold, or something that might be worse.

What concerned Carolyn more was the bruising reality that to Brian almost all bodily functions were an indiscretion. He loved her in his own way, but his grasp of human intimacy had yet to mature beyond adolescence. She knew some of this before they married but it all seemed pardonable at the time, given first that a long-standing hometown beau announced his engagement suddenly and second that a rival younger sister had married someone worse.

The time had come to marry, and she married him.

In his late teens, Peter's mind was consumed completely by human rights on one hand and by self-interest on the other. In college classes or debates with friends, he argued that his resistance to the Vietnam war was driven largely by pacifism and, more generally, by his parents' politics, campaigning maniacally for Adlai Stevenson in the '50s and for JFK in 1960. But politics aside, he was frightened immeasurably by the photos he'd seen in *Life* and *Look* magazines and by footage nightly on the evening news. Self-interest trumped pacifism hands down, although rights consumed him on other issues, like voter suppression in the South. Peter had a sincere interest in voting rights and a dim view of elected state legislators who read to their advantage the Constitution's provision that voter qualifications be determined by the states.

Peter had wanted to march in Alabama but didn't. He'd wanted to join sit-ins in Nashville and the Student Nonviolent Coordinating Committee thereafter but didn't. And he'd wanted to meet the art student activist who shared his anti-suppression instincts. This he did. Laura Steinberg became both his political soul mate and his first serious love. In late summer, four years after they met, the Selective Service draft looming on the horizon, Peter and Laura married, granting Peter the exemption he needed and the freedom to pursue law school.

Hardly the best reason to marry, but they did.

AT THAT POINT IN A LETTER WHERE prose turns to pillow talk, someone who's flipped for someone younger would do well to avoid the Postal Service than to drop in the mail a permanent record of their over-the-top devotion. Everyone knows this. Peter didn't know this.

"I'll be at the Drake the Sunday after Thanksgiving. About 2 p.m. Hope you're free. Be great to see you." Fair enough. No overreach there. But then he concluded with "I miss you." This broke new ground.

To have written that crap down, he thought, soon after mailing the note to her, looking out his office window toward the row of leafless trees standing tall over two coeds facing each other, hands clasped between them, their faces smiling for reasons, he guessed, that had everything to do with abundant joy. There they were—he'd seen them before—out in the open, visible to anyone who'd care to observe, enjoying the freedom of public affection the era had only begun to allow. Oh sure, Carolyn had complimented him—*You look great,* she'd said weeks before—but compliments have the shelf life of milk.

Shit, he murmured—though no one heard—overwrought with thoughts that conflicted badly. On one hand, he feared he'd committed an act unpardonable of a mature adult, much less an educator admired by a wife—by all accounts, loved by a wife—but a wife he'd been finding tiresome. And who was he to find *anyone* tiresome. He was the one handcuffed by a shyness that gave everyone in Peter's and Laura's orbit reason to regret their invitations. On the other hand, people for millennia have caroused with one another with little thought to who might get hurt. And Carolyn certainly had begun to suppress his shyness. *Shit or get off the pot,* he'd said more than once, though never before to himself.

Two weeks later, Carolyn replied in a note she mailed to his faculty office. "The Sunday after Thanksgiving is booked for a special man. (Looking forward!)" She apparently understood the power of parentheses—and Peter understood he was off the hook.

Thanksgiving came and Thanksgiving went, both for Peter and for Carolyn.

ON A CLEAR, UNSEASONABLY WARM AFTERNOON, Peter boarded a flight to Chicago, where the air was cooler, the clouds dark, and the wind gave signs that winter was near. Entering the Drake's crowded lobby triggered for Peter a childhood memory of brief Sunday visits to his grandmother's house on the way to afternoon family road trips—a happy place to gather oneself on the way to someplace happier. He approached the front desk to check in.

Front? Oh, Mr. Correnti, you have a message. The desk clerk searched an expandable folder. *Here it is.*

Peter took the note in his outstretched hand and slid it unopened into his pocket. He was confident. The way we act when we're about to be in the company of someone we're certain admires us. Unopened? Why hadn't he opened the note? For one thing, he didn't want to appear overanxious, either to the desk clerk or to himself. But for another, he knew that whatever Carolyn wrote would be welcome. And good news is nice to look forward to.

Minutes after settling into the junior suite, Peter opened the note. "I'm dropping Brian at the airport," it read. "I'll call from your lobby." There was no outward sign of affection in the note, although who would add affection to a cryptic message dictated over the phone? No sign of bad news there. Besides, "dropping Brian" wasn't meant to discourage him.

When the room phone rang, Peter felt composed rather than hopeful, calm rather than anxious—a change from the early fall.

Hello?

Peter!

Carolyn. You in the lobby?

You bet.

Great, I'll be right down.

Peter looked close in the bathroom mirror, quickly dry shaved whiskers on his cheeks, and wiped fallen stubble from the marble sink with a hand towel he folded and returned to the shelf. He checked to assure that the room was tidy, took one last peak in the foyer mirror, then closed the door behind him. He entered an elevator with a woman and a child. He smiled at the woman and she smiled back.

The elevator stopped and following a pause—a long pause, Peter felt—the door opened.

Carolyn saw him first. *Peter, it looks terrific!* she said in a startled though unmistakably approving voice.

Thanks.

It's nicely shaped. A good look on you. You've had one before?

No, but why not? Winter's coming!

Did it itch? My father's did.

You know, it didn't, although I played with it a lot during the grubby stage. He raised his head, a gesture that signaled a change in subject. *But the grubby stage is over now …*

… I'll say it is …

… and I'm ready for a drink!

Me too, she said. *How 'bout a place I know on Rush?*

Sounds great.

In the cab, he raised his arm over Carolyn's shoulders—a risk, but her saying, *I'll say it is,* gave him the excess capital to spend. Carolyn leaned into him and, facing ahead, she smiled. Promising moves all the way around, although Peter's arm felt awkward held high on her elevated shoulders and progressively heavier as the ride wore on. He had no choice but to tough it out.

The lounge seemed to Peter an adequate setting to stage the night's next step—secluded, dark, and sufficiently quiet to prevent their voices from carrying. He felt more comfortable than he had in the cab, although the table he chose was uncommonly large—maybe even too large for two—leaving more distance between them than he thought the evening required.

Good Thanksgiving? Carolyn asked.

Mostly, he said.

How's that?

You heard about the Vegas fire?

Sure, it was all over the news. MGM?

Right, Laura and some friends cancelled a trip for that weekend, the weekend before Thanksgiving. One of them got sick, so they cancelled.

Was she shook up?

Sure was. Is.

I'm so sorry.

They weren't staying there but they'd have gone. Everybody does, she said. I can't imagine. People in elevators, trapped. Heat, smoke. In an elevator!

She okay in elevators? Carolyn asked.

No.

You?

Not always, he said. *That's why the Drake. Ten floors I can handle.*

Admitting a weakness was attractive to Carolyn. Withholding a weakness is one thing—like Brian's, say, from her in the past—but admitting weakness early in a relationship was, to Carolyn, a sign of confidence. Peter sensed this. She was wrong, he knew, but he went with it.

Elbows on the table, leaning in, their conversation grew more familiar, then intimate through eye talk and stares.

Guessing he wouldn't, she spoke first. *Brought that Chardonnay we liked—the Kistler?*

I thought your bag looked heavy, he said.

She opened the bag to show him the bottle. He saw the bottle—and a wallet, gum, the head of a toothbrush. *Go back and try it?* she asked.

You bet, he said.

They were less talkative in the cab, her on her side, him on his, hands by his side this time. The blur of buildings, street signs, and lights seemed to make no impression on them. Neither one spoke.

They walked past the doorman—*Good evening, sir*—and into a lobby elevator.

I loved this elevator as a kid, Carolyn said.

This? This elevator? Peter asked.

Right. It's one of the ones with a bench they've got that my aunt let me ride after lunch. Birthdays she'd take me to the Coq d'Or. Shirley Temples, the works.

From the elevator, they walked to room 834, a number Carolyn looked at closely. Had she been here before?

Peter fumbled with the key, turned the doorknob, opened the door, and followed Carolyn in. If you'd lingered briefly in the outer hall, you'd have heard in succession the fuss with coats, the pop of a cork, a laugh or two, inaudible talking, then mumbling that faded to silence.

DURING THAT PERIOD IN ANYONE'S LIFE when the transition to middle age appears, the body softens, lines form, hair thins, and there's never again the mistaken call to a young man or young woman. Peter thought these things on the eastbound train to Boston's South Station, where he'd planned to meet a co-author on a new commercial-statutes manuscript in search of a textbook publisher. They'd gotten some encouraging feedback, but knew they needed a renewed strategy, an angle that distinguished the manuscript from the prevailing competition—a pithy catchphrase or focus-group data that might persuade a publisher, any publisher from Peter's point of view, his promotion to full professor hanging in the balance. Train travel was simple. There'd be time to think.

And he did think. About Laura.

She'd transitioned too, but she welcomed the gray she found in her hair, accepted that drinking less was prudent; and resigned herself that, having faced long ago that she wouldn't have children, the time had come to mentor children. Art in a neighborhood school, perhaps, or after-school guidance in a community center. He'd seen this in her—was impressed with her—but lamented the unwelcome disconnect among the onset of aging, a wife who embraced it, and his infatuation with a younger woman.

And oddly, he came to think about railroad stations, although this didn't surface till a stop in Framingham, where he saw through a window the nineteenth century fieldstone station, witness over the years to countless scenes of reunited travelers returning to someplace or someone cherished—a family, a loved one, a childhood home—from world wars, Korea, Vietnam, or from distant colleges and universities. Airports held memories far more recent but seemed decidedly different to him, dominated as they are by commercial travelers peddling their wares, plotting deals, swindling counterparties in contract disputes.

Academic life had insulated Peter from commercial woes. But it hadn't insulated him from a secret diversion he found himself preoccupied with. Rather, it gave him time to think, time to concoct his vain deceptions. The hidden-motive business trips and boldface lies, both of which were dramatic contradictions, insults even, to the grace Laura showed in the face of maturing—and, for that matter, more time to think about the Framingham station, this very station, where she welcomed him home from an ethics board hearing he'd never revealed his role in.

Two weeks later, on a weekday morning, things took a turn for the worse.

PETER REACHED FOR HIS VALISE, stepped out onto the parking lot pavement, and strolled to his faculty office building, playfully dragging his chukka boots through shallow piles of fallen leaves. He passed the iconic music hall, then climbed the steps of his building. In his office, the light from an east facing window cast decidedly distorted shapes in shadows elongated by morning sun—knick-knacks transformed into candlesticks, a coffee cup into a pot or an urn. But Peter's attention was directed elsewhere. He had things to do, among them energize his book proposal. But first, he took a gluttonous bite from a bagel he'd brought from home.

The office phone rang suddenly and unexpectedly, as all phones do, but particularly so when our cheeks are bulging with tough chew. On the fifth ring, he answered the phone.

Correnti, he said, standing, chewing.

Peter, it's Carolyn.

Carolyn. What a surprise! Say, can you hold a minute? Just a minute.

I'll wait, she said with no inflection, no sign of excitement—and this was exciting. Her first call to his office.

Peter dashed around his desk, closed the door, hurried back, and juggled the phone in his clumsy hands. *Sorry, I just …*

Peter, your gift came.

Oh? They said it'd be shipped the nineteenth. The nineteenth, it would ship. And it's only …

Peter, I can't accept it.

He was wounded. He'd bought a Christmas gift for a woman who preferred he hadn't. *I thought you'd like the sweater, and the skirt's ….*

Peter, I don't think of you that way.

Peter was stunned, his senses numb. He was forty-two years old and felt no different than he had decades before when a cheerleader said much the same thing.

But Carolyn, I thought …

You thought what?

He didn't answer.

I'm sorry, Peter. I don't mean to hurt you.

The word "hurt" gave him an opening, a chance to say something personal. *I am, Carolyn. I thought we were on the same wavelength.*

I thought we were too.

By now, the sun was higher. Shadows cast truer images on the floor. He was sitting at his desk, head titled down, eyebrows raised, sweat building.

Peter? Like before, her voice faded. An awkward silence followed.

What Carolyn?

I'm sending it back. To you.

Please keep it, Carolyn. As a friend.

I can't, Peter. Please don't ask. I'm sending it.

I'm sorry, Carolyn. I misread.

You misread? she said, her voice now pitched to the resounding tone that injures on impact and humiliates over time.

WHAT IN CAROLYN'S ADULT LIFE had been worse than this indiscretion with Peter? Certainly, the urgent but fraudulent phone call she'd made years before, claiming her mother had been seriously injured, thereby staging an excuse on day two of a bar exam she knew on day one she was failing? Or the abortion she planned in New York in college, unable to admit, even to herself, that the boy might have been a classmate's father?

Panicked, she navigated both those things.

Older now, she'd navigate this indiscretion—and navigate calmly, precisely because, all things considered, this one wasn't worse.

Laura Correnti's home phone rang. *Hello?* she said.

Mrs. Correnti?

Speaking.

This is Brian Pitts, Mrs. Correnti. You don't know me. Your husband knows my wife.

Yes?

Is this a good time?

Yes.

We're from Chicago, Mrs. Correnti, my wife and me. Your husband and my wife met here last summer. They've met here since then. You didn't know that Mrs. Correnti?

She didn't answer.

Mrs. Correnti?

Yes, she said.

You didn't know your husband was seeing someone?

She stood there frozen, both hands gripping the phone's receiver. She didn't answer.

Mrs. Correnti, I'm afraid …

Laura Correnti hung up the phone.

Brian Pitts hung up the phone.

What did she say? Carolyn asked.

Nothing, really. Hung up, he said.

CAROLYN WAS FACING ARRESTING STRESS from the onset of symptoms she kept to herself. She withheld from the doctor some early signs—nausea, cramping, tender breasts—dismissing them as routine. Then kept from Brian abdominal cramps, discharge, and bleeding that suggested something worse.

Tomorrow morning, Carolyn answered.

How 'bout I go? Brian said.
You haven't before.
He'll scan this visit?
Ultrasound, she said. *But I'm not sure they'll let you in.*
He smokes, for Christ's sake. <u>He</u> won't let me in? Brian said.

Brian was seated at a kneehole desk, head bent over a checkbook and pen. Across the room, Carolyn stood at a bay window, watching a misty October rain. She left it at that, said nothing more, and drove to the morning appointment alone. The ultrasound confirmed what she suspected. She listened half-hearted to the obstetrician, drove to a pharmacy, got what was ordered, then drove home to cry. She'd tell Brian later that night, after he got home.

Carolyn had learned to cope with stress by reminding herself, time and again, that nothing she'd do, ever do, would be worse than what she'd done in the past—plotting a fraud on the bar exam, carousing with a classmate's father in college. Those were bad but comforting now since she'd gotten away with both of them. No one suspected her audacious fraud or that miscarriage precluded a trip to New York. She was young then, consumed by the burden of facing alone systemic guilt that, if she'd been caught, she'd never live down, partly because of grievous acts and partly because she had lied. The two acts were troubling; sure they were. But live with the memory, she reasoned in time and, going forward, rely on the memory—leverage the memory—as a means to cope with whatever goes wrong, unless the wrong is worse.

Worse, this?

No, not this.

She slept better than Brian that night.

WHAT ARE THE THINGS CAROLYN said that Peter remembered most? *A special man,* he remembered that. *A good look on you,* he remembered that too. But nothing more powerful than the punishing line, *I don't think of you that way.* Maybe from a movie or something she read? More likely, though, all by herself, not unlike the spontaneous insights and penetrating clarity that impressed him most at first.

He'd searched her occasionally over the years and saw online that she'd distinguished herself. Fundraising for the facelift of an historic building, a local small business leadership award, and an e-book on Amazon that caught his eye, *Quick Books for Lawyers*, or something like that. Her web presence was inconclusive, but Brian's gave every sign that the two were together. Claims to a spouse named Carolyn, who was listed as an occupant at the same address. And prosperous. The address carried an online, estimated value well north of his own. But no claims about kids that he could find.

The thought had plagued him for years on end and then he concluded, why not? Given the number of years that had passed, hadn't time offered the distance sufficient to reach out innocently? Just this once, after all this time? Don't people search for people they knew and then send a hoping-you're-well hello?

He found an email—she was working still—and composed carefully what he thought would work. A brief note that stayed above the fray. Nothing personal—"just reaching out," something like that—something that appeared gracious and caring but wouldn't reveal the utter truth that, to this day, he's reminded of her almost every day. For instance, she told him that rinsing a cup in scalding water holds the heat in the coffee longer, prompting him often to do the same. And the oldest daughter of a practicing dentist, she brushed her teeth every which way and then she brushed her tongue, something he'd never done before, prompting him daily to do the same.

He prepared a draft in Notes on his phone. "Hi Carolyn, just reaching out after all these years, hoping you're healthy and all is well …" Preoccupied for days—thinking, adding, revising; thinking, deleting, revising—he drafted an email he knew was safe. Detached, objective, cheerful, brief. Nothing that crossed the line. Nothing effusive in any way. Something he'd write to a former student who'd distinguished themself some way. "Just reaching out to say hello."

He thought about it for several days—thinking, editing; revising, thinking—then hit "send" with no reservations at a respectable time on a work-week day.

It didn't bounce back.

He wasn't belabored with guilty thoughts that he might have overreached. He had been in the past, but he wasn't now. He'd done what he'd wanted to do for a while. Nothing he said could be misconstrued. Something almost anyone could read and not think anything untoward. His conscience was clear. The ball was in her court.

Now to wait.

To give her time to collect her thoughts. To think over what she would say.

You Sure This Here's the One?

I make the time to visit my mother, living now in a third-floor walkup, climbing stairs with a force of will she'd groomed through years of fending alone. No one wants to probe these things, but I'd put it off too long.

Give me another month, she says when I say, *I think the time has come.*

I change the subject to change the mood. *Come on, let's go for a ride,* I say.

Sure, she says. *Let's go,* she says, relieved as me that the probing's done.

Despite the slick December roads, we drive the city much of the day, stopping first at the Cup 'n Saucer, where I stand in line at an open counter, reciting her order in my head. She's seated at a four-top set for two, safely removed from counter staff she'd been given over to mistreat badly if her order was wrong in the slightest way, like lettuce dangling over a bun or coffee in a mug too hot to hold.

Today, a far less common day, her order arrives entirely right—cheese melted, *Not too much,* pickles placed where pickles are placed, *If dumbbell cooks are on the ball.*

Back in the car, back on the road, I drive by places she should have known—bus stops, buildings, parks, streets—hoping to get her memory going, hoping to hear her words flow, hoping to see what she remembers. A test, of sorts, for both of us.

Oh sure, she says, passing a costume jewelry shop that hired her after my father left, getting us through the everyday of rent, food, utility bills, and a landlord happy to saddle us with heat that trickled from a single burner in an aged oil stove. *Look!* she shouts, pointing to the double door by the shipping dock where she'd enter mornings and leave at night. And *Florence,* she says under her breath, the forewoman who forgave her when, late to work, a friend clocked-in for her. *No one else got away with that, the times I had to do it,* she says, a startling admission from a mother who resorted to a form of cheating that she would have punished me for.

Well, she says, *I'm not sure, no,* when we pass an all too imposing building, once a long term care facility with steps I climbed to visit my father after he left the house for good, after he'd been committed, she said—to an all too anxious, frightened child who could only imagine what "committed" meant—then died the way she'd said he wanted, suffering in silence a sapping depression the era didn't allow in men. She lived with my father—loved my father?—but respect for him was another thing.

Remember dropping me off? I asked.

No, she says, *I don't.*

I told her I had a two-hour drive to a stop that night for a morning call. Really, I wanted to be alone—alone to do what I couldn't do, not with her in tow. Truth is, we'd had a good day. For one thing, she seemed to remember more than she had on recent visits home. For another, she agreed to a month or so and understood that the time had come.

A pretty good day, today was—all the way around, it was.

I dropped her off, gassed the car, then drove to visit my boyhood home.

A RAMP THAT RISES FROM A CONCRETE WALK to the porch I played on as a child cautions me to take my time climbing the steps to the wood front door to knock then ask if the occupant, maybe, would let a stranger visit the house he lived in years ago. Like a summer day, a warm day, when a man in an Air Force uniform asked the same of me and my mother, who sent me off to the grocery store with a list a mile long.

I knock on the door, a woman answers, and I lean forward to ask her.

You sure this here's the one? she asks.

Let's see, I say. Brown not gray—wasn't it gray?—in a row of identical double-deckers, each with a porch and three-step stoop, most surrounded by a chain-link fence.

Scanning the houses—left, right, across the street—I could see why she would ask. I step back, look, then pause longer. Sobering—it was, I tell you—that I had to pause to recognize the house where I grew up. But comforting, more or less, that years had passed since I stood on this porch.

Folks mess up, she says to me. *Even some who live here now!* That was comforting too.

I say, *It's the one.*

She laughs.

We gab.

She invites me in.

The door seems smaller than I remember but has the same imposing deadbolt—and a shiny new bolt mounted below, a telling sign that time had changed the neighborhood.

She opens the door to the part of the visit made more for gesture than for speech. I point when I see a narrow pantry, where my mother stood and washed cloths. Is it longer now than it was back then?

I smile when I see a kitchen range, like the one she lit to boil water to avoid an otherwise ice-cold bath. Oh my, the joy of a nice warm bath after a hot water tank was installed, after my sister left for good or maybe before she did.

And I stare a bit, stuck in place, when I see the room where I worried so, conspired alone to cheat on tests, and felt the fancies a child feels when growing up takes place. So many years since I'd slept here, heard the yelling that came to blows, felt the anguish a young child feels when parents spill the vile language unheard by the child outside the home. The worry in this one small room and the realization, years later, that none of the worry accomplished much—if even I can remember now exactly what I worried about.

Then to the door where the changes came.

I neither point, nor smile, nor stare at the door that led to my parent's room, before it became my mother's room, after my father moved away, before my sister slept in there, after my sister's pregnancy, before I saw my mother less, after her memory began to fade—just as I know that mine has faded earlier than hers, I'm afraid.

Where This Was Going

I stop to spend the coming night in an aging one-star motor lodge that wouldn't bust per diem. Nervy to give it a star at all but one star isn't saying much. A travel guide I saw in a rack at a limited-service welcome center didn't list a single place that didn't have at least one star.

I decided to check-in here for the night, since I'd heard of the bar next door.

Good move bringing food from home, allowing me to save some time and to file a meal-reimbursement voucher below the amount accounting says needs a written receipt. But bad idea guzzling beer the night before a sales call the boss said, *Could be big.* I did drink hard when I was teaching—before and after class, both—but I found that drinking on a sales call was a risk of a different making. Wiping it off your breath's the problem, knowing a prospect's standing near. Students, at least, you can keep your distance—them pinned down in rows of desks.

Sending you, the boss had said—and said at times to any of us when he thought we'd think he'd done a favor. He wouldn't cut-in on a sales commission, but you knew you'd owe him other ways. Like looking away when he cut corners—on maintaining company cars, say. I hadn't planned to drink so hard the night before a call, but the kids were at my mother's tonight and casing the bar when I sat down, a woman alone was walking in.

Poised and assured, from what I saw, she sat on a barstool two from mine.

She seemed to wear her confidence well. I'll say that for her.

Upright on a backless stool, no side glance that I could tell, and a top and jewelry, both well matched, except for a pendant strung from her neck—a brooch with a star, like the place I'm at—that seemed to fall too low on her, not unlike my daughters' do when they wear their grandma's necklets. Her jacket, folded and set on the stool, sat her somewhat taller than me. No harm there, someone taller, but taller than her would help a bit if she tends to think like my first wife, screaming, *Shrimp,* when she walked out, at the top of her lungs for all to hear, including a neighbor out in the hall.

I finished the beer I had in hand, then moved to the seat beside her. Forward maybe but who's kidding who? You come to a bar alone at night and don't think that might happen? I could have motioned her toward me—like they do in forties film noir movies—but for one thing, this isn't a staged plot and, for another, my strength is more in conversation than in what my ex called, *Average looks.*

I bought a round, she bought a round; me again, then her. Pay by-the-round is the custom here. At least that's what I'm seeing. Maybe the tabs got skipped too much. We drank each round with little talking. Far too little, if you ask me.

The small talk seemed too small to me this far into the beer. I needed to move the pace along. Say something personal enough, but not too forward for now. There's always a risk.

Nice brooch, I said.

She looked at me, straight at me.

The shape, the star, I said pointing. The color of the star matched her eyes. She smiled, I think, or smirked.

A table? I asked.

Fine here, she said to me, looking ahead, straight ahead, maybe at herself in the wall-mount mirror that stretched the length of the bar.

Looking down, avoiding her eyes, I took the liberty to say my name. *Don,* I said.

She looked at me, one eyebrow raised, like TV news reporters do. *What?* she said.

Don, I said. *They call me Don.*

Oh, she said and that was that, as if she would have guessed different or thought that I meant something else. I've heard "what?"—sure I have—but never "oh" in all my years of saying my name to someone else. Nothing came back from her on hers. I wasn't sure what might come next, so I took to doing what I sometimes do when the lay-of-the-land's unclear. I took the subordinate position.

Yours? I asked. *Your name,* I said, angling for an answer.

She didn't look back. No gesture, smile, frown, or glance. Didn't say a single word—to me or anyone else, she didn't. Instead she stood, glass half full, brushed her jacket of lint or dust, and walked straight out the door, no word.

I should have seen where this was going. Nevertheless, the buzz felt good—and at half the price, well worth it. I ordered another, threw down a tip for the bartender—a youngish guy, who'd had the sense not to look, even when she went strutting out—and left through the door the woman did.

Back in the room, belly full, I watched the news for the next day's weather, mulled over wasting breath in the bar, and peed what seemed like more than a minute. I laid down heavy on the double bed and felt the well of sleep set in.

I was out.

The night, until then, went just like that.

Then I woke a few hours later in a way that up and startled me. Heart racing, a pool of sweat, the room off balance, spinning. That's happened before when I drank too much.

This time I felt different. My arm seemed far too deep in sleep to be an arm asleep. No sign yet of the pins and needles when a sleeping arm wakes up.

I touched my arm, grabbed my arm, pinched my arm. Dead and limp as kneaded dough, longer than just an arm asleep. I got up from bed to get some water. Helps to thin the blood, I'd heard, to make the heart pump slower. First step, good; next step, good. Steady on my feet, the walk went well. No dizziness, lightheadedness, brain fog, or confusion.

As a test, I recited in the room out loud a passage I taught in school. *I do not know what it is about you that closes and opens* ... Don't know now, it's been years. Elliott, maybe? Cummings? *Only something in me understands the voice in your eyes is deeper* ... So far, so good. *Nobody, not even the rain* ... I spoke right through, no hesitation. I felt no different than I had before, the times I overdid it.

I recited no more. I didn't need to. There was no problem in my head. The trouble was in my arm.

I sure didn't want to be an alarmist, but I don't mind saying I was alarmed. Who do I call for advice on this, lacking a doctor to call my own? And how would I face my calculating boss—or, for that matter, my worrying mother—if, in the end, this all blows over? These things blow over mostly, don't they? Something, I guess, that comes with age or the weight of a looming sales quota I'd yet to make so far.

It seemed like I should stay awake. Walk a little, stand. Until this went away, at least. Just in case, like a wife would say if I had a wife to say it. That call tomorrow, I'd need the sleep. I needed to stay awake, though. Not let myself get worse in sleep and not wake up to catch it. They say there's signs, warnings, markers—things to make you pause and think.

I did pause. I did think.

I thought good thing that woman left. And then about the kids.

How Could I Get Away with This?

Returning on a bus from a second-run screening of the first *King Kong*—my interest more in the undressed damsel than anything having to do with Kong—I'm struck by a woman across the aisle, her face obscured by a turned-up collar and a scarf that gathers beneath her nose. A hem at the bottom of her camel coat is frayed from a brace the coat let show and an iron stirrup above her ankle reflects at intervals flicks of light that ricochet-off aluminum panels, seemingly mimicking Morse code taps, like the *RKO Pictures* opening scroll.

Nothing of the flesh above her knees is otherwise exposed, not with all the buttons tight and both hands clutching the top of her coat.

Then looking up, I'm struck far more. Her collar down, the scarf released, I can see she's looking straight at me, eyes directed square at mine, making clear she knows. She knows that I've been staring at her—my attention to the brace and the iron stirrup having persisted far too long to pass for a passing glance. She caught me dead to rights, she did. But looking at my guilty grin, she could not know that, able now to see her face—my glasses pushed up from the tip of my nose—I'd forgotten the bus, the theatre, the movie, the coat, the hem, the brace, and the stirrup once I saw her pale blue eyes and the beauty mark God drew on her chin.

Not much more than a few days later—a weekday after-noon in fall—the face of a most familiar girl startled me in the Department of Records, the topmost floor of City Hall. Metal stairs, peeling paint, imposing photos of the city's heroes, belied the warmth and gentleness I detected in the smile on her face—not unlike the smiles I'd seen around her locker, near the gym, and in our school's dining hall.

Not on her face for me, this girl. Not for me, not her. But well within plain view of me. Day after day, most days at school—though not, till now, outside of school.

Three grades older, long blond hair, a face as pure as a por-celain doll, and light blue eyes like the woman on the bus, the girl was sitting at a desk I'd approach for directions to access archived records I'd tell her I need for a school report—on family births, marriages, deaths—she'd likely done herself before. A part-time after-school job, is that the reason she's here just now? To the job do I owe a tip-of-the-hat for the chance to approach her all alone? I didn't know and couldn't tell—and could hardly ask a girl like that. A girl who looks as good as that, a girl I didn't know.

I approached her desk real slow, knowing that—guilty that—there was no family-tree report. I'd made that up for her. Rather than need, I *wanted* access to archived records to find the obit of my baby brother, deceased two years before I was born, who my mother said died of an unknown cause and my father said nothing, like he often does. Not for nothing, but am I to believe that the cause of my brother's early death is entirely unknown?

He was two years old. No one keeps track of a two-year-old?

If only I could speak to anyone else—a career civil servant, a pimple-faced boy—anyone other than someone I feared was bound to tie my tongue. When does it happen that we come to fear impossible, arresting attractiveness? When does it happen that we come to suspect that our mother has taken to lying to us—in this case, a mother who demanded I attend, against my will, a school that trafficked in the knowing truth of an omnipresent God she knows? She might know, but I'm just coming around to know.

Indented marks on the bridge of my nose, formed by a pair of horn-rimmed glasses, could expose a flaw I was loathe to show. Which is to say nothing of my other flaws, among them knowing that I couldn't look older than I really am, absent lifts in the heels of my shoes and layered T-shirts under my clothes. To compensate, I walked up close, glasses off, to talk toward where her eyes would be, hoping she won't know.

The ruse went well. Or fairly well.

She walked me back to drawers of records stacked in a sea of metal cabinets. She found the records I pretended to need and turned to point them out to me. *Here's where you want, the years in here.*

Wait, what? I can search these drawers myself?

Yeah, she said.

I can read them? I asked, realizing the words were right but arranged pitifully wrong.

Yes, she said. *These ones are back far enough that they're public records under the law. Leave 'em on the table, the ones you take. We'll file 'em back when you're done.*

I looked at her. "These ones"—is that what I heard this goddess say?

Like the library, I said, hoping for a laugh, a smile or, failing that, maybe just a simple shrug. No dice. She looked away, turned toward the door, and disappeared into the hall, releasing me to reach for my glasses—as if she'd care what I do.

An approximate date of death in hand, I fingered through rows of 3x5 cards—most scribbled-out or typed or printed— for a few days before the date I had and for a few days after. Bingo, a record that offered detail, though nothing on the cause of death—"unspecified, natural" is what it said. Most surprising, the record attached a brief obit from the local paper reporting that an afternoon wake would be held at our address.

Our address?

The very address where I huddle at night, watching with my parents our TV set, and nary a word from either of them—not one word, not once ever—on what went on in there once?

Where in the room was the pint-sized casket? Aren't wakes held in funeral homes?

When does it happen that we come to know to take the good with the bad? In this case, the bad that came to good when I learned in the course of scanning the records that whatever it was I suspected of my mother—neglect, maybe? a dreadful wrong?—wasn't recorded for public consumption, relieving me of the gnawing fright that the public knows what I don't know. Oh sure, no cause of death is puzzling, since that's what I was looking for. But scanning through some other records, many said what my brother's said, offering me the degrees of freedom to leave City Hall relieved. If this wasn't liberating, then what does the word liberate mean?

I turned from the drawers of filing cabinets, left the room, and approached her slowly from a sideways angle—a chance to stare at her in peace.

PLAGUED BY SHAME FROM AT LEAST TWO SOURCES—a demanding mother, furious nuns—I endured alone the nagging sin of thoughts I knew indecent. How could I get away with this, when an all-knowing God already knows of behavior nuns were prone to call nothing less than molestations? That was the word they used, those nuns. Good God, my God, molestations? Not in deed, not so far. But I had sinned in another way. What Sister called a steppingstone— the altogether disturbing thoughts that seduce weak-minded boys. About this, Sister seemed to know.

My devotion to the faith, even as a child, was entirely residential—who, growing up, does not take first the faith of the family around them? And part of the faith where I resided would insist that I confess. If she found out, my mother would demand no less, since the faith offers no other option—this from a mother whose demand for herself was attendance at Mass on Christmas Day, though no other day that I could tell, not even Easter Sunday.

I'd done this before when my mother pushed but never once made a true confession to anything other than minor infractions I figured a priest would buy. *I lied to my mother,* was my go-to sin—not really a lie, truth be told—but, given what had been worrying me, I was saddled with colossal guilt for sins I thought pure vile. Sins that *were* pure vile.

I swear a lot but that's not it.

I've cheated on tests but that's not it.

I'm obsessed with women and girls. That's it.

There, I said it. I am. I admit it.

Everything tells me this can't be good. *Don't think about girls when you're alone,* Sister said, her constant mantra when she had the boys corralled together. But I *did* think about girls alone—all the time, especially alone—and, worse than that, I thought about girls out in public, like standing at a desk in City Hall and riding in a crowded city bus.

Everywhere really, and anywhere at all.

What was I to do? Me, a child who kept to himself, prompting a counselor to tell my mother, *His energy comes from an interior self.* No way I wanted to confess to a priest. Isn't it enough to confess in prayer at home alone, under my breath in silence? Isn't that where interior is?

I relented. I had to. No other way. I had to confess these impure thoughts out loud in the presence of a parish priest, partly for a reason I'd long been taught—the forgiveness only a priest can bring through confession that serves to cleanse the soul—but mostly for a reason I kept to myself. Rather than later, now on earth, God could disable my wayward eyes, *Punishing you for good*, Sister said.

Already, I needed these damn glasses.

On a Saturday over Christmas break—raising the risk of gifts at stake—I walked to the bus stop in heavy snow, rode past the stop at City Hall, and paused alone to catch my breath at the top of the church's imposing steps.

Bless me, Father, for I have sinned, I practiced in silence, kneeling at a pew awaiting my turn, and said aloud in the confessional stall, kneeling before a crimson curtain, my confessor behind an opaque screen, hidden and out of view to me, except for his head in silhouette, obscuring his identity.

My confession was detailed, emotional, pleading, and even let slip I knew full well that, if I don't come clean before a priest, God may levy my suffering on earth, long before I get to hell.

My mother, I said. *Unfair of me. A sin, what I thought— and something that never happened.* From there I went where I wanted to go, the sin that brought me here to him. *Girls*, I said. *Women*, I said. *Girls and women, anywhere. A feeling I feel in front of them—or by myself, alone.* I tried to imagine how to explain what the feeling was. Things in my head. Urges that hadn't been there before. Feelings unfelt near anything else. *Bless me, Father*, I said instead. *For I have sinned*, I said.

Surely, he got what I mean by now. A little action from the priest, maybe?

His pause was long. His head behind the screen still. Then he whispered, *Three Our Fathers and three Hail Marys.*

Really?

I couldn't believe that's all he said. For penance, for this? For sins I thought secured my fate to burn in hell, where Sister said with high conviction that mortal sinners surely go. Goodness gracious. Not so bad!

Maybe it's best you see me later. After weekday Mass, he said. *Break this week,* I think he said. Christmas break, I'm sure he meant.

Waiting at the bus stop, standing alone, sitting on the bus, walking the sidewalk to our home, I felt an uncommon, prideful joy returning with my soul wiped clean of a sin I couldn't get out of my head—till now, I couldn't get out of my head. Wasn't this a joy to share? A joy to share with my parents?

Of course it was.

A priest, I said. *I can't defy a priest,* I said, pleading to my parents when I told them both that untold sins had been forgiven at Peter in Chains Church—not our parish, not for a while, but the church where I'd made my First Holy Communion and where, at last, a priest had enlisted a forgiving God to pardon my grievous sin. I'd confessed to a priest, been forgiven, been invited to visit him later, and shared the news—though not the confession—with a father and a mother who'd introduced a path to redemption that only a priest in a church could give. I looked at them, they looked at me.

The two of them sat and listened.

Which priest? my mother said.

I don't know, he didn't say. The one who'll do morning Mass on break. I didn't smile but intended to smile at the first sign of a smile from them.

There wasn't a smile from either of them.

My father and mother sat rigid, tense. Hardly a thing came back from them, other than nods and, *Go on,* from her. A moment later, they dismissed me from the living room, sat together on a three-cushion couch, and spoke alone in soft whispers. From where I stood—in the kitchen, the hall; pacing, sitting—I could see them both, him in a cloud of cigarette smoke, her with hands raised to her face, their expressions oddly contorted, puzzled, prompting the question in my mind, *What made me think this would go well?*

Later on, darkness falling, they called me into the room with them. *Never again,* my father said. *Never again, that church,* he said, both hands gripping the arms of his chair, a cigarette dangling from the side of his mouth. A wonder for him to say that much.

Listen to your father, my mother said, a tissue in her hand. This was a surprise for my mother to say.

Sure, I said. *Okay, sure,* saying out loud what they wanted to hear but not what I said to myself. *Rarely attending church themselves, how the hell were they to know?*

III.

None but the Most Diminished Hopes

1.

Three times a day, an air horn blew two short puffs then another one long, signaling a change in eight-hour shifts and arrival in the street of an overflow crowd, half shuffling in, half heading home. Most dragged and flipped near the entry door or lit and dragged in the crowded street. Lucky Strike, Camel, Old Gold, Pall Mall—none with filters, not back then.

All were decked in work boots, goggles, soft hats, gloves, and company issued Eisenhower jackets to fend off knife beds, rollers, pullies, or a boiling spill from a wood pulp vat that the father said, *Eats deep into the skin,* partly to share what the mill was like and mostly to scare his son away. The boy took pride in his father's job—*Head mechanic,* he'd boast to the kids—at the Crosby-Kent papermill, the largest employer on the town's east side, and pride in his role as co-head usher at a church in the shadow of the red brick mill.

The boy could tell—he'd heard kids say—that the mill was the dream job of teenage kids. Finish high school—they knew they should—enlist in the service for a three-year hitch, return to town, apply at the mill, save what you can, and marry. The father had higher hopes for the boy, like a high wage skill—commercial heating?—and slack in the hours he'd have to work. The mother just wanted him to grow up happy. *Who can love who isn't happy?* she said to the father, stroking the young boy's buzz cut head after something the father said.

But she died before she'd see if he did—*Advanced cancer,* the father said—a crushing blow to the young boy who, before her wake at his father's prompting, signed the guest-book for both of them, a memory he'd cherish for years to come. As a child and later as a high school kid, the boy wanted what his father had. Five days a week, eight-hour shifts, weekends free if the shifts went well, and a short walk home at the end of a shift to houses built after the Depression and maintained later by veterans proud to own them.

In time, the boy hired on at the mill, his father notwithstanding. He worked second shift in maintenance, then moved away when, except for a crew that included his father, the mill moved south to exploit the promise of cheaper labor. By a stroke of luck, the boy—a man, you could pretty much say—found a couple of towns away another steady good paying job managing collections and past-due accounts at Coro, Inc., a metal findings and stampings plant whose receivables department the Army depleted through a draft the Congress rebooted that year. Lacking any relevant experience—he'd worked with his hands like his father did—he fibbed a bit on his Coro application (high school bookkeeping, senior year), was willing to learn, and would. His father distrusted paperwork and loathed the men who'd stoop to it but knew not to argue with a check coming in, his hopes for the boy growing dim after the boy's wife left him.

This has to end, the boy's wife said. Or he thought she said when, bags in hand, she abandoned him without a word on why she did, allowing him to evade the weight of all he knew she meant by "this." When they first met on a weekday night at a bar in his new neighborhood, each cast an image that swooned the other. Her green eyes greener than the bluest green; his shoulders broad, his hair thick. There wasn't much else to their mutual attraction, other than how the other one looked—a brief turn real and not so real, qualifying, his father said, for erasure by annulment. *I liked her, though,* his father said. *Good there weren't no kids,* he said, offering the boy a cigarette.

The boy took a Lucky from his father's pack, held a match for both of them, then nodded his head without a word.

A YEAR OR SO INTO THE MARRIAGE, a letter came to deliver news. Anything coming to the boy or his wife came for the other one too. Like news that an inquiry absolved him fully of absconding with company cash receipts weighed as much on her as him, since she'd taken his last name as hers. And news that internal bleeding had ceased precluded for her a delicate surgery and for him the anguish of untold cost in the face of limited insurance.

They'd dodged some bullets, Carmen and Adam. Whatever was coming, each of them knew.

Then this.

No word from her that something was coming. Thinking back, he realized that weeks had passed since she'd said much of anything to him. Didn't say she planned to cut her hair. Didn't say she joined a fitness gym. Didn't say she quit her weekday job managing a laundromat that doubled in the practice of payday loans. Hair and a gym were no big thing, but didn't her job bear on him? There had been subtle changes in her that suggested something was coming, something that might be big. A startled look when her cell phone rang, quick to her screen when an email came, and first to the mail the last few days, even in pouring rain. Clearly, something was on the way and, despite her silence, there could be news for him.

Rather than dwell on what was coming, he dwelled on what to bank on.

He'd bank on faith—faith alone—that the news would turn out good. The faith his mother instilled in him attending church on Sunday mornings, gifting food to parishioners suddenly out of work, paying at some sacrifice Adam's parochial school tuition. No two ways about it, this was a wholly faithful boy. But his outsized faith was a rub for Carmen, right from an unexpected night in a cheap motel they'd found by chance driving in a bleak Nor'easter. Squinting groggy from the bathroom sink, she gasped out loud when she turned toward him. Hands folded, head bowed down, kneeling beside the bed in prayer. Alarmed that she'd become unglued—*What are you, a child?* she said—he took thereafter to saying his prayers one knee down by the bathroom sink.

He didn't know, she didn't say, but he figured she'd be thinking luck. Luck for whatever would soon be coming. Faith had little place for her. She'd endured eight years in parochial school, reading scripture a teacher said disciples drafted decades later in a language—Greek—they didn't speak, let alone write, casting doubt on dogma that prevailed ages later. It didn't matter if this were true; it was what she wanted to hear at the time and what she argued to her zealous parents. They said, *Faith, not fact,* to her—though, very much to Carmen's surprise, her argument prevailed. She enrolled in a neighboring public school where the only cross she'd see again was the one above her parents' bed. That was enough of that for her.

She'd bank on luck. It figured she would. The luck that had evaded her, confessed in a bar when she said out loud, drink in hand, that Adam was the one she settled for, a friend told Adam Carmen said.

Neither Carmen nor Adam spoke of this. Not in so many words, they didn't. Faith for him; good luck for her.

That was part of the difference in them.

She entered the apartment, a letter in hand. He looked at her. She looked away.

She opened the letter, making no effort to hide from him the word she'd been awaiting. She stood there silent inside the door, out in the open in front of him. Just one page, the letter was, but she took her sweet time reading. Too much time, it seemed to him, for nothing more than a single page. No gesture, look, or word to him. And no expression on her blank face after reading the letter again. Instead, in silence she closed her eyes, breathed in deep a breath or two, opened her eyes, walked to the bedroom, letter in hand, and closed the door behind her. He heard some scuffling in the medicine cabinet, then nothing other than cold silence.

That was part of the difference too.

The cabinet was, that is.

Adam stood near their bedroom door but didn't dare go in. Instead, he wondered, pacing alone, what his mother would have said, if she had lived to say it.

IN GRADE SCHOOL, MID-MAY BROUGHT the joy of Adam's favorite day of the year. The day his mother would call the school to report at once his absence. Should the call have been one too many, a truant officer—the school department's resolve in hand—would begin the parade of horribles. A knock on the door, a surly look, a decree to witness an ailing child. This was her first call in months. She had budgeted wisely.

The truant officer kept at bay, Adam stood on the porch alone, squinting to see oncoming traffic, then called to his mother when he saw their bus arriving. The one that read "Downtown" in front, not the "Express" that, boarded in error, would blow through town to the state capitol, crowded on board with government workers and riders en route to the state's best shopping.

Ma, Ma! It's coming! he called.

They were on their way, a fourth grader and a well-dressed mother, each one smiling ear to ear.

Downtown held a trove of treasures they'd visit in roughly the same order on this one day—hooky day—in the Spring of every year. Fluffy, three-egg Denver omelets, elbow to elbow at the Modern Diner (*Stuffed!* Adam would tell his mother, tapping his distended belly); licorice from the counter at Acorn Books, steps from a shiny manhole cover (*Don't trip on the cover,* she'd say to him, *or step on the date—bad luck, it's the year I was born!*); pay toilets at Shartenberg's, one floor up from a toy display (*Wait for the free one,* she would say; *Just one toy!* she'd tell him, smiling); and then to the hands-down highlight of the day. A stroll on the banks of a narrow millrace—built in the late 1700s—that propelled a giant waterwheel, creating the power to drive the looms at the Jedediah Wilkinson Weaving Mill, an artifact of the town's past that, despite the industry's migration south, ran two shifts each day.

Adam, she said, standing beside him, the waterwheel now in view. *Let's stop a minute,* she said to him, holding his arm with both her hands. *Close your eyes, breathe in deep, then breathe in deep again.*

He did.

Now listen.

Listen to what? he said.

To what you miss when you're busy looking. Just stand there and listen.

Okay, he said, both eyes closed. *Water in the river, I guess,* he said.

What's the sound, the water in the river? What's the water sound like?

Ripple ... rippling ... the gurgle, gurgling ...

That's it, she said. *What else?*

Water flowing, smacking the bank. I can hear that too.

What else? she said. *Other than the river.*

He closed his eyes, scrunched them tight. *Wind in the leaves, birds in the trees, cars over there ... a baby behind us!* He opened his eyes.

See? she said. *More than you hear when you <u>are</u> looking!* She smiled at him and he smiled back. *Now, let yourself forget what you're hearing—and listen to what you're thinking!*

Smile gone, Adam was puzzled.

Thinking? he said.

Sure, she said. *Like, want to know what I'm thinking?*

He nodded his head.

You go on to the waterwheel! I'll sit here and catch my breath.

He smiled, began to walk away, then broke into a full sprint.

The wheel was a wonder to the grade school boy, a bewitching relic of yesteryear—and it was in every way. The way the wheel stood tall in the race, spilled water on the trip around, and gleamed like silver where the mid-day sun struck paddles, bolts, an axle, troughs—unlike any Ferris wheel could. The spinning, swirling sound of the wheel, newly imagined from his listening drill, was faint from a distance as he approached, then powerful as he drew near. And the pungent, metallic, cold, wet smell that told him he'd drawn near enough.

Did you see how drops of oil from the gears color the water beneath the wheel? she asked when Adam returned.

He said he did—*Bluish, yellowish, bits of green*—but didn't say what he also saw: legs flat out, her color pale, beads of sweat above her lips, hands on the ground supporting her weight, dark stains lurking under her pits through a fancy top that seemed to him light enough for a warm spring day under the shade of a stand of trees. She *had* kept pace, stride for stride to Acorn Books and Shartenberg's, but not on the walk to the waterwheel. She had in the past but not this year.

The spectacle of the waterwheel—the majestic height, the sound, the smell—played out to the enchanted boy like fireworks on the 4ᵗʰ of July. Puppeting what his father had said, he'd explain why fireworks did what they did—*A fuse and a shell at just the right height*. And explain, as well, what a millrace was—simply, maybe, but you got the idea. *The narrow part of the water stream that the narrowing makes run faster*. He had suspicions, but he couldn't explain why the stroll had winded his mother, wiping a start-of-the-day smile off her end-of-the-day face.

Sitting on the shore, Adam told his father, *over near where the Totem Pole is, she let me walk the length of the race*, further than she had in prior years. *I was almost out of her sight*, he said.

Bent over, was she? the father asked. *A cough?* he asked, clearing his throat, holding a cough of his own in.

A little, I guess. More the sweat. The sweating.

Did she stop to go to the ladies' room?

Not then, no, but later she did—before we got on the bus, she did.

Drafting a past-due dunning letter to the venerable Wilkinson Weaving Mill, Adam thought about all of this. And thought, too, about his mother's funeral guestbook stored in a drawer beside his bed, cluttered with entries from every-one—relatives, neighbors, co-workers, friends.

Love wants most for signs of love.

Is that what his mother would have said?

WHAT ARE THE MOMENTS IN CHILDHOOD that announce to a child they're growing up? A child aroused by physical change, vaguely aware of what was coming. A parent consciously navigating silence, keeping secrets from an innocent child. Or something else arriving to a child otherwise unexampled by itself.

Glancing idly between his knees, Adam was startled by smears of red on the upper lip of the toilet bowl. Some light, some dark, some darker still. He leaped from the seat con-sumed with terror, bent at the waist, eyeballs bulging, and inspected himself everywhere he could. Everywhere private that blood could gather and not be seen, even by him. He pulled back skin from the head of his penis, positioned a mirror to see his rear, and swiped a ply of toilet paper along his rear where he couldn't see. He looked where he could, wiped where he couldn't.

Nothing, not even a vague pink.

Satisfied his body was clear, the sweat on his head subsiding, he inspected the toilet as close as he could to assemble clues that would lead him to the bottom of this. Kneeling at the toilet, hands on the rim, he positioned his head by the toilet bowl rim—inside and under the porcelain lip that circled the top of the bowl. Blood?

Inspecting the rim all the way around, he was sure as his untrained eyes could be that the smears were remnants of someone's blood. Of this, he thought he was almost sure.

There were notes of color on the toilet bowl rim—some pink, some red, some almost brown—making plain that someone tried, surely tried, to clean the blood they spilled. A lot of blood, he was pretty sure.

And how long since the blood appeared? And what would cause blood to spill from someone in the house who wasn't him?

He thought to himself—*Do I run and ask my mother and father?*—then arrived at a better option, sparing himself the lies he'd hear. Surely, it had to be one of them. And if it was, neither would tell him who had bled—if either had told the one who hadn't.

He walked from the bathroom to the eat-in kitchen, and toward where both his parents sat, side by side at the kitchen table. They turned toward him. They'd been talking—he could tell they had. He could tell when they stared up at him, rather than continue what they'd been doing.

Wash your hands? his mother asked.

I did, yes, Adam said—though he hadn't really—to see what else she'd say.

A lot of rain, his mother said.

The last few days, his father said.

Rain, Adam said for something to say.

Time to get ready for bed, she said.

He left the kitchen without replying, went to his room, closed the door, and positioned his ear flush to the door, hoping to hear what he could. There was silence from the kitchen, apart from the sound of chair legs shuffling and talking he wasn't able to hear, partly due to his distance from them and mostly due to untimely rain that muffled the talking he might have heard. Something was up. He was sure of it. His queasy belly told him.

Minutes passed.

Ten minutes, maybe more—him standing, leaning, ear to the door. Their voices were reduced to mumbles, whispers. Then all of a sudden, a slam on the table and two raised voices, some of it clear.

Jesus Christ! his father said. Then something else that wasn't clear.

Drive for hours? ... his mother said ... *Bald tires* ... he thought she said ... *Kid in the seat behind us?*

Kid?

He'd not heard his mother say "kid" before—but who was the kid, if it wasn't him?

My God, the father said to the mother.

The rain let up, but he heard no more. Faint talking, nothing clear. He abandoned the vigil at the bedroom door, climbed into bed, and lay awake, prone position, an arm extended to the hardwood floor. They were keeping something important from him. Something to do with one of them, with both of them—or if not them, then him. He was sure they were.

SOLITUDE HAD A WAY WITH ADAM, even as a child. He reveled in play as a preschool kid, though mostly all alone. He'd play by himself with miniature soldiers, tanks, and trucks or comics he'd cut from the Sunday paper to display in a cutout cardboard shoebox—one frame at a time, like a crude TV—as if a morning TV show was playing in slow motion. He couldn't read what the "bubble words" said but, not unlike an offstage voice, he'd shout out loud what the pictures said. *He's fine,* his mother said to herself, fretting often when he gave no sign of being lonely, even when kids were outside playing. In time, she came to realize, *Adam's a boy with an imagination,* she said to his father, bereft that a boy—a son of his—might never learn to get along. Adam presented—to his mother, at least—as a boy in a world that he imagined, an unambiguous sign of ruin to a father who attributed his own self-worth to where he stood with men in his midst.

Though not to his father soon enough, Adam began in second grade to display a newfound appreciation for activities he couldn't do alone. He discovered the wonders of roughhouse play. This he couldn't do alone, offering a welcome sign of progress, both to his father and to his mother. Any sport, or version of a sport, that carried the lure of physical contact fit the bill in spades. Like soccer, where rules disable hands but tripping is more than common. Or basketball, where rules forbid striking a player, but elbows, knees, and an errant hand are weapons to deploy in earnest. And football. Ah, football. A chance to block, tackle, and shove without the corresponding risk of breaking the rules of the game.

Adam was becoming a bit more social—no doubt about it, he certainly was—but aside from football, basketball, and soccer, Adam preferred to play alone. If he did play with neighborhood kids, he preferred to play with one at a time. *Go out and play!* his mother would say, repeatedly say in second, third, and fourth grade. *There's kids your age outside,* she'd say—and then say less in fifth grade and ceased to say by sixth grade.

Around the time that puberty began to rage in young Adam, he engaged in behavior easily hidden by a reticent boy. First, on Cub Scout merit badges, though it took some time to build the courage to bring himself to cheat. The lure was irresistible, mostly because a Scout uniform was all the rage, worn to school on meeting days, attracting the glances of other boys—and some of the girls Adam's age. Who could resist the grandeur of a Navy blue uniform, a bright yellow neckerchief, and a brass-plated neckerchief slide? The neckerchief, *Now that was something,* he told his father, who reluctantly shelled out hard-earned cash for a costume he'd have cherished as a kid.

But scouts were expected to complete tasks and submit reports, leading to sew-on merit badges that, once achieved, graced the uniform, chest and sleeves. Take the Insect Merit Badge, a circle patch that framed an insect Adam thought a sign of menace. Most of the requirements were fairly simple, like an introductory paragraph explaining parts of an insect's body. Easy enough. Just paraphrase from an encyclopedia. But some of the requirements required work, lots of work, like observing outdoors twenty different living insects and describing each in detail. Twenty? For this, he returned to the encyclopedia his mother had bought, one volume at a time, from a local grocery store promotion. He prepared the report in a single day, then waited about a month or so before presenting the completed project. Submitted in the dead of winter, insects long dormant, the Den Leader, a kind woman, looked the other way.

Oh, he felt the nagging pangs of guilt—an upbringing in a faithful home, a mother who'd never cheated on a thing, a father who'd say he hadn't either—first, in the lie his report had been and again and again on other badges. On the other hand, the compulsion to complete tedious tasks with little more than minimal effort was much too hard to resist, particularly with a father at work most days and early to bed most nights. Who would see, if his father didn't? Over time, in the coming years, much of the guilt would fade away, since solitude shields perverse behavior, an unexpected benefit to a boy who relished time alone.

Worth the risk?

Worth it.

2.

There were signs that Adam wasn't over Carmen—his appetite, the drinking. Or wasn't over what he knew she knew—or, if not knew, suspected.

Back before she'd left for good, they'd gotten behind on several bills, like a TV they had bought on time, rent on their apartment. Nothing big alone so much but enough together to floor them. Then suddenly Adam could pay the bills. *All in full,* he said to Carmen, who came to learn, to his dismay, that Coro commissioned an inquiry—a first step, an intrusive step, before a full investigation. He'd drafted and sent a past-due letter to none other than Wilkinson Weaving, a balance that Wilkinson's management said they had paid promptly. Prepare one, sure—that's routine—but mailing the letter could blow his cover.

It did.

Nothing Carmen had experienced with Adam predicted this from him. She was pissed. Coro's management hit the roof. Wilkinson was outraged that a payment cleared, *The bloody bank,* but hadn't reached Coro. *Your oldest account, you don't call first?!*

Skimming a book Adam bought to hone his woeful accounting skills, he came across a promising scheme. Heist a customer's incoming check, endorse the check to your own account, then cover the heist and forgery with an equal-or-larger incoming check—a seemingly easy scheme. He'd navigated the fraught gymnastics needed to keep the records straight—heist, forge, repeat; heist, forge, repeat— but he hadn't figured that having failed to remain alert, the first rule in a checking scheme, he'd placed the letter in outgoing mail, rather than in a locked drawer. A colossal, self-inflicted blunder.

Adam was at a loss for words.

Handled by Coro's accounting firm—a stretch, the spectacle of an outside firm, but this was the fabled Wilkinson account—the inquiry concluded, albeit naively, that rather than an embezzlement the matter was a simple clerical error. No need for a full investigation. Wilkinson's check having cleared his bank, Adam made a deposit to Coro's account, recorded the deposit to Wilkinson's credit, and hoped they wouldn't notice.

They didn't. He'd headed 'em off, voilà!

Like Adam and Carmen had done before, he dodged a bullet that, unlike bills he couldn't pay, would have driven damning ruin, not to mention a prison term had Coro filed a criminal complaint.

I was absolved! Adam said to Carmen.

Bullshit, Carmen said to him.

The accounting firm ...

Just out of school, the accountants they sent. One, the kid of a woman at the gym. Lucky for you, they're dumber than you.

You don't believe me?

No, I don't.

I've prayed on it ... Adam began.

... No hypocrisy there! she shouted, releasing a source of her contempt. She reached in her purse for a cigarette, for something to do with her hands and lips.

Absolved—he was, he was in the clear—Adam nevertheless understood the gravity of his sin. For now, he'd bask in the utter relief that only Carmen presented a risk.

He got into bed long after her.

Rarely redeemed in moments of insight, he turned toward Carmen to inhale again, if never before, the oscillating warmth of her oncoming breath, missed altogether in the everyday, as anyone misses anyone's breath, for all we see that seems more there, like signs she wouldn't stay with him in any way like she had before—stark precursors to a bitter end.

He slept poorly, ate alone, left home early, and then, after a full day's work, texted Carmen to meet at a bar. They did.

Each sat tall at a two-top table, hands by their side, call brands set before them. Bud for him, Cutty Sark for her. He'd taken the time to primp for this—a moment in the mirror, tucked-in shirt. He could tell she hadn't.

Knowing she held the upper hand, Adam began by easing in. *What was that you said, I think, you came to Cutty how?*

She looked at him, then blotted her lips with a cocktail napkin. *My father, he drank nothing but. All there was to sneak.*

How old?

Told you, maybe twelve, thirteen—whatever age you come to notice it's fun and it's forbidden.

That age, you didn't gag? he said.

You figure the buzz is worth it, she said. *Told you this before.*

He shifted cheek to cheek in the chair. *A year this month,* Adam said, sitting in a bar much like the one she'd told him they were pregnant. They were "they" at the time she would have told him. *Isn't it?* he asked when she didn't answer.

Don't go there, she said.

What?

You, caught with your hand in the till and I should answer to you?

I didn't have a say?

No, you didn't. My call, no one else's.

Adam had hoped the look in her eyes would slip back into time—back to the bliss when they first met—but instead they reflected his flaws and blunders. He sat defeated, hands on his lap, staring down at an empty glass, aware of signs that, quite apart from years before, her boredom with him was far more potent than her taste for him had been.

THE TROUBLE PEAKED WITH ADAM and his father when the father started saying things. Things his mother, before she died, taught him never to say or think. Now the father was saying things—crude, vicious, startling things on what he saw or said he saw, *Everywhere in the neighborhood*. Raging rants, you could almost say from what the father was saying. Rants that Adam would not repeat. He took at first to ignoring his father. Then, as the words grew more vulgar, he couldn't listen to his father anymore. He'd leave at once for his own apartment, until he thought to leave for good or at least till this blew over.

Months later, on a visit home that Adam's conscience demanded of him, he saw that the rants had ended. Dressed in only his underwear, nails curling over his toes, the father sat in a leather chair, an open pack of Kool cigarettes on a drop-leaf table beside him. The father sat with his head held down, didn't open his mouth to speak. Instead, he scribbled on a scrap of paper. "Trot herts," the scribble read—a clue after all these years that maybe his father couldn't read? To what lengths had his father gone to keep his long-held secret?

Signing for his father his mother's guestbook, was that a clue back when?

Adam made calls, waded through a maze of lengthy options, and arrived later at a live voice that served him with compassion. He drove his father to a VA hospital—"Kent" Memorial, of all things—waited long for a scheduled appointment and through a battery of diagnostic tests, then listened as the doctor explained to him the prognosis wasn't good. A throat gone raw from sores and welts left the father in agonizing pain. Adam knew then that, months before, he should have listened to his father more.

In his father's day, cigarettes occupied idle hands much like phones would decades later. Some knew the harm that tar unleashed but thought the risk worth taking. Add to this, if it's not enough, the toll that working in the mill took. No one sheltered their vulnerable lungs from fibers the saws spewed cutting sheets the workers milled into stock-keeping units, one for reams of control-line paper, supplied with pride to area schools and poached by workers for their children's use, making the workers celebrities at home, even with pre-school boys and girls who couldn't write with confidence yet, their pencils locked up in befuddled hands fated to operate paper machines their parents' accumulated scars were from.

Didn't help, the doctor answered. *But plenty of people present like your dad who hadn't smoked or worked in a mill.*

Will he go home? Adam asked.

The doctor said he wouldn't.

His mind drifting when the doctor left, Adam recalled that he learned to smoke from his father's example—long pulls on the day's first drags, fresh packs tapped on the back of your hand to tamp down loose tobacco. And learned to write and to draw well too on Crosby-Kent control-line paper, the lines a guide for depth and proportion in pencil sketches of all sorts of things, including features of a paper-mill. Calendar stacks, parent rolls, wet felts, winders, drying machines—all of which he'd sketch in detail, enlisting the aid of Polaroids and what he'd seen in the nearby mill.

His father sedated in critical care, Adam drove back to his father's house to gather clothes for the coming night, an air horn blowing aloud in his mind—faintly, maybe, he's a grown man now, but enough to revive his memory of the horn, mornings after his father left and evenings announcing he'd soon be home. Sun near dusk, he parked the car and walked the streets of a neighborhood that had ceased to resist the signs of decay. Vacant now, save for drifters and roosting birds, the four-story Crosby-Kent building was a skeleton of its once proud self. Only an occasional newspaper clipping bothered to mention the long gone firm—in obits, mostly, written proudly by workers' children, just like Adam would write himself. Machines long gone, jobs long gone, scrub obstructed a chain-link fence employees painted to a silver gray that had given way to a rusty brown in an area stripped of the neighborhood pride that returning post-war enlisted vets impounded into their homes and yards.

Walking alone on the empty street, weeds thriving in a shattered curb, Adam scanned the boarded building and the pavement darkened from rubbed-in tar, remnants of mountains of cigarette butts where, years before, workers walked on the same pavement, all their secrets held within. Was his father able to read enough to protect him from suspicion? After all, his crude spelling of "throat hurts" captured the sound of the words well.

Though fully absolved of a blatant fraud, the initial wave of joyous relief had given way to crippling shame that hovered tangibly over Adam—maybe no less than his father felt, holding his own secret in. Does shame play out about the same in the minds of those who live with it? Are all our secrets almost the same? Plagued as he was with riveting guilt, there was no way that, even as a child, Adam would have asked his father this.

Standing where his father walked, he remembered his father's morning cough, the sound the boy would awaken to, until falling numb to the weekday rite that preceded his father's daily commute to a timeclock near the mill's front door. He remembered his father's morning voice but remembered more the hacking cough. Not the first out-of-breath cough that signaled the barrage about to come. More the second, deeper cough his father ceased to make an excuse for. In the second cough, he could hear the wheeze the mill made his father make mornings at home—and the gurgle, deep in his father's chest, like the gurgling waters of the Tiler River he'd heard with his mother years ago.

FOR YEARS ON THE BANKS OF THE TILER RIVER—and much more now, more recently—locals complained that something was wrong, dreadfully wrong, with the once vibrant river. Decaying fish, paper, cans, and all manner of plastic wrappings littered the nearby banks of the river. But this wasn't the source of discontent. Far more troubling in summer months was the sudden appearance of a soapy foam, so unexpected on any river, inciting a city-wide commotion. Odious odors somehow aside, foam shouldn't float on a healthy river—and certainly not in airborne foam balls aloft in force on breezy days when gusts of wind were sufficiently brisk to launch the foam on adjacent streets.

The scent of decay was bad enough, but unseemly foam drove days of talk in diners, bars, grocery stores, and letters to *The Evening Call*—one from a woman bombarded from behind by foam balls to her back and head—an increasingly contagious local outrage plainly galling to passersby, to laborers in adjacent mills, and to tenants peering from open windows, some two blocks away. Unemployment was rife in the city, but political ads would have you believe that nothing mattered more to voters than the pitiful state of the Tiler River.

Standing at the millrace he'd visit as a child, returning after his father's death, Adam remembered his mother's reminders to witness the array of vibrant colors adrift in the narrow race of water, beneath the historic waterwheel that today churned a soapy foam afloat where the wheel entered the water, presenting like a brackish brine, and feeling in the mist on his shaven face more like oil than clean fresh water. And the smell was entirely different today. Not the cold, metallic damp he recalled from visits in his wide-eyed youth but dank, putrid, rancid, strong. He'd returned to the millrace to reminisce—to relive visits he'd made with his mother—but from what he saw, nothing was right with the once grand river he hadn't strolled on foot in years.

A five-mile-long tidal extension, blessed upstream with natural falls, the Tiler River nourished livestock, residents, crops, and powered mills along its banks, beginning with the millrace Jedediah Wilkinson dug and dredged to accommodate a waterwheel—the source of power to a weaving loom that Wilkinson assembled from private blueprints he'd witnessed in England months before. Other mills followed suit—paper, cable, ironworks—signs of rampant industrialization that harnessed power from the river's falls. For two hundred years, give or take, the natural course of the Tiler River sustained an explosion of industrial investment and proved a continuing source of power, fishing, and recreation, attracting workers, farmers, visitors at accelerating levels of rampant development the river couldn't sustain. Not anymore, it couldn't.

Pollution had prevailed.

Leaning on a rail above the millrace, aghast at a scene so unexpected, Adam didn't know what to make of this. He'd heard a report some nights before but passed it off as political banter, recalling the role as a natural resource the falls and the river had always been. Today, the river was an abject shame, a blemish on an idyllic memory that seemed to mimic the discontent river towns suffered nationwide and a reminder of the role the abandoned papermill played in the decline of his neighborhood. Even the church he'd attended Sundays lost its thriving congregation, closed an adjacent grammar school, and consolidated pastoral services with a parish facing its own doom.

Adam wasn't raised in an activist family—complaints, sure; action, no—but driving back from the Tiler River, energized in a brand new way, he concluded that, arguably for the first time ever, he'd arrived at a cause to probe. In fact, a cause he *would* probe, given that he had time on his hands. Laid off from Coro's receivables group—the job now required spreadsheet skills his boss could tell were over his head—Adam moved back to his father's house where, as his father's only heir, he'd taken title on his father's death. For now, he'd live on his father's savings, bide his time, and take up the plight of the Tiler River—an homage to what his mother would say if she had lived to say it.

Is there any difference between the living and the dead when the dead empower novel behavior? Thinking this, or something like this, Adam, raising a comb to his hair, smiled wide in the bathroom mirror, the only joy he'd felt that day—the joy that his mother would approve of this.

OTHER THAN ONCE TO HIDE FROM THE RAIN, Adam hadn't walked the marble floors of the Eleanor Meade Public Library, not even as a kid. Not what kids in the neighborhood did—or what you'd have them see you doing. To read indoors, or anywhere else, was hardly tempting to young boys bound to the wonders of outdoor, roughhouse play—including Adam, who'd otherwise prefer to play alone, except for football, basketball, soccer or games like "muckle," which became Adam's hands-down favorite. A made up game, one boy only, football in hand, scrambling to avoid the incoming tackles of every one of the other boys, all of them on defense. No rules and certainly no objective other than avoiding nasty tackles—neck locks, knee chops, swipes to the groin.

Think young boys, piles of boys, bent on exacting screams and pain.

Driving to the library, he thought about his hardnosed play and about the chance he would have predicted years ago that he'd one day pass up everything else to go instead to the public library. *No chance,* his youthful self would have said.

He parked the car, approached on foot the Classic Revival library building, glanced at the row of ionic columns and the classic egg-and-dart molding—neither of which he'd have noticed before—and climbed two flights of stone steps to walk through a set of double doors to read what recent editions of *The Evening Call* reported about the Tiler River. Opening the heavy entry door, he was overcome with the awkward sense of a place off limits to a man who, despite his age, had never once read a book clear through. Not even the books assigned in school—not completely, never. A shame quite like the crying shame of his botched, get-rich-quick checking scheme suddenly overcame him. With power, the shame came over him. He walked through the front door anyway.

Sky-high ceilings, granite walls, and imposing books on metal shelves belied the warmth and gentleness Adam sensed in the smiling, *Help you?* releasing him from the nervousness he felt when walking in.

Sure, thanks, Adam said. *Back copies of The Call—The Evening Call?*

Yes, we have them.

I've been away, Adam said. *Saw the Tiler River's failing. Thought there'd be some coverage in The Call.*

Has been, yes, a series—front page features, some of them.

Looked online. Couldn't see much, a paywall.

Of course, yes, let me show you.

The two walked back to a spiral staircase, wound around a supporting pole that climbed with the staircase and pierced the ceiling, giving way to a musty room, piles of dailies stacked in rows.

Here's what you want. We store six months in the stacks, here, then send them out for microfilming. The feature pieces should be here.

Great, thanks, Adam said.

Let me know if you want back further. Microfilm's downstairs.

Sitting alone at a long oak table, Adam glanced at piles of *The Call,* wishing there was a quicker way, like someone he knew to ask, say, relieving him from the burden of reading. But for one thing, kids he'd known in the neighborhood had long since moved away. For another, the generation before him—folks who'd be his parents' age—were mostly in their graves. No other way. He'd have to spend some time reading.

Adam scanned the prior night's paper, then back each day, one by one, pausing at notable one-off pieces on retiring teachers, plant closings, high school scores, obituaries. Even those pieces were a chore to read, a signal to abort this boring task, till he sat straight up, eyebrows raised, having arrived at an article he likely would have overlooked, had a full name not been set in bold.

> *North Bend: A driver was arrested for cocaine possession and driving while intoxicated during an investigation into a crash on Saturday, according to the North Bend Police Department. At 10:40 p.m., deputies were called to the area of Japonica Street and Broadway. The driver, identified as* **Carmen Monti**, *age unreported, was found to be under the influence of alcohol. K9 Bear was deployed to Monti's vehicle and alerted to the presence of narcotics. A field sobriety test determined Monti's blood alcohol level was three times the legal limit. Monti was booked on operating a vehicle with a BAC of 0.15 or more and possession of cocaine. Monti was released on bond.*

In the days after his father's death, Adam placed Carmen firmly behind him, partly because her departure was final and mostly because she failed to attend the funeral or the wake. The wake, okay, maybe not, since she'd see Adam face to face. But back of the church on the day of the funeral, was that too much to ask? The article, so unexpected, brought Adam back to their early days, back to the days when news for one amounted to news for the other one too. Didn't that weigh on her? Not on her about Adam so much but how about his father who, although he'd refused for Adam in his youth, had been the source for Carmen's bail, and maybe more, well after the marriage failed but before the arrest reported here?

No worries, Adam told his father when, long before the rants began, his father confessed, voice shaking, that he couldn't bear to leave Carmen in jail, *Not when I came to understand. God forgive her,* his father said. *God forgive me,* Adam thought he said.

Carmen didn't solicit favors. She found it fruitful to identify an obliging mark, build trust then sympathy, bide her time, and wait for the mark to volunteer, just like Adam's father did. Having learned her arrest appeared in *The Call,* he reached out to Carmen's public defender, arranged bail, and met her later in a coffee shop, where she happened to mention, out of the blue, a procedure his father said she said, that his father knew his conscience forbid. Ambushed by her sobering tears, he offered to help her nevertheless, interpreting the help—to himself, at least—as indemnification for neglected duties he'd come to feel in arrears to. Wouldn't news of his father's death have reached her in some way?

And now, from the piece in *The Call* before him, she'd found herself arrested. Adam placed the paper on the chair beside him, rather than back in the stack it came from. Minutes later, he hadn't looked at another edition. Adam had to find her.

In a huff, he'd deleted her cell from his phone. Indifferent, he'd discarded Carmen's address and ignored her friends' last names. He had no presence on social media and didn't know if she did.

Put everything back, Adam said, approaching the ground-floor desk.

Thanks, can I help with anything else?

Well, yes, if you can, he said. *How would I find an arrest record?*

Depends on where the arrest was made. Some you get at the courthouse, there. Some you get online. You know the jurisdiction?

North Bend, he said.

*They're online, if I'm not mistaken. Would you like to check?
Here?* he asked.

Sure, I'll show you.

They walked to a bank of public computers. Adam logged on with a daily password, fumbled through a clumsy search, and stumbled on a record.

*Arrest Number: 22-55759-AR
On 10/07 at 23:14 hrs., officers arrested Carmen Monti …
22 Washburn St. #2,
Wickenden*

. . .

He'd find her.

ADAM HADN'T SEEN CARMEN SINCE SHE LEFT—and thought to himself, for a fleeting moment, that maybe he shouldn't now. But longing obliges reckless behavior, like cavorting with an ex who, come to find out, concealed drugs, harbored secrets, and invited risky bouts with the law. Each one a reason to remain in place, were it not for the bouts of longing. Dressing for the drive to her address, he tried to avoid a shirt or a coat Carmen might have seen him in. Tough to choose from the clothes he had, since he had so little to choose from. He had no will to pretend he'd prospered. He wanted to signal that he'd moved on—*this* in case, with the passing of time, she hadn't moved on either.

Adam drove in heavy rain, found her street, sat in the car, then set up shop in the Friendly Tap, a bar in view of her front step. He thought better of approaching her door, risking she wouldn't open the door. Better to greet her on the street—in full view of passersby—where her reaction was likely to be restrained.

Soon after dark, the rain now passed, a car pulled up—two women? a woman and a man?—and Carmen stepped out from the car to the curb. Adam placed cash on the bar before him, stood, and walked across the street. He wanted a chance to talk to her—or wanted to want, at least.

Standing alone on the concrete curb, Carmen fished through her coat pocket. Adam crossed the narrow street, avoided a puddle, and approached Carmen from her rear.

Carmen, he said, nothing more.

She turned, saw him, and didn't speak.

Talk for a minute? Adam asked, his smile forced but giving no obvious sign of aggression.

If you must, she said.

The bar? he asked, one hand pointing across the street, the other scratching his long, predictably close-shaven face that, although sturdy in the jaw and cheeks, appeared to carry sagging flesh—maybe the beginning of the middle-age jowl his father had bequeathed to him.

Fine here, Carmen said, her face youthful or seeming to be. Had she weathered well the drugs and drinking? But something was different about her voice. Hoarse, maybe— maybe that was it—an artifact of the heavy smoking she'd started as a kid?

Read about the accident, he said.

Uh huh, Carmen said, removing her knee-length overcoat, revealing a full-figured silhouette—a shape he once called hourglass fit—that somehow looked to have changed in ways more likely a sign of weight than age. The curve at her waist had disappeared and her chest protruded no further than her waist, despite a nylon cinch belt that couldn't have been pulled tighter.

How'd it turn out?

Suspended sentence, she said to Adam, his shoulders strikingly wide still, as if he were wearing shoulder pads. Once thick and wavy, his hair had thinned, making his head seem somewhat smaller than you'd think at first those shoulders would rate.

Look, Carmen …

I've moved on, Adam. You need to.
It isn't that.
What, then?
My father, he helped you …
He told you? Carmen interrupted.
Right, he did.
Told you what? she asked.
Helped you out, that's all, he said.
Bail, she said.
I know you've got a new life, Carmen.
God sake, she said.
All I meant …
She looked away.
We had some falls, he said to her, knowing that "we" might overreach.
My falls all came natural, she said.
He didn't reply. He knew not to speak, knew what he'd said was beside the point—"all I meant," "a new life," "falls"—but something came out anyway. *What happened…,* he started to say, then stopped in his tracks, startled that she had squared-up before him, inches away, her manic, piercing blue-green eyes looking at him with all there was that was in her to look.
No one gets, who doesn't bother, that this isn't something that happens to you! Veins appeared in her forehead and neck.
His weight shifted to his heels from his toes.
Seeing this, his subtle retreat, she stepped back, turned, and walked from the curb to her front door, holding her head up most of the way.
Carmen, he said loud enough to invite a glance from a passerby. Rather than answer or stop or turn, she quickened the pace, Adam could tell, and entered through her unlocked door, keeping to herself what he couldn't tell—keeping what's best left kept secret.

WHAT DOES THE OCCASION OF returning expose? Returning to the house where Adam grew up, to an ex remade into someone else, to a river stressed into rundown ruin. Each one exposed a mystery, though not in equal measure. The house was a home surrounded by blight and Carmen an obsession somehow fraught. But the river, the millrace, and waterwheel held captive Adam's imagination for reasons that were unknown to him.

Kneeling in a house now his own, he felt a subtle flash of warmth, dampness on his forearms, palms, and face—a strangeness he'd felt at times before though had only begun to grasp the shape of. Having reached the point where preoccupation made the turn to gripping stress—it had; he felt it brewing on his skin—he'd do what he knew he should have done and likely what his father had never done. He'd reach out to someone.

Ten stone steps, three brass rails—the same comforting steps and handrails Adam had used on Sunday mornings—led to the pews where parishioners sit, forward to the altar where clergy roam and, if you knew where you were going, to the Sacristy where priests held court in Mother of God Church. Adam's boyhood church. And lest he be haunted by shades of guilt, Adam's church today, more or less. Early by minutes for a morning appointment, Adam entered the Sacristy office that read COME IN on the outer door. Might this be the reception area? Adam didn't know since, having reneged on a childhood promise to become an altar boy, he'd not proceeded this far before.

Hello, he said in the empty office. And, *Hello?* again in the form of a question, then lost the courage to say more. He sat.

He was minutes early and, he thought, not too late to abort consulting with a parish priest who, on the silver anniversary of his ordination, revealed at a celebration Mass that his parents were sitting in a pew upfront—unlike Adam's, fully alive, breathing on their own—and gave no sign, when acknowledging family who supported him, that his past included a wife's rejection. Nothing at all like Adam's life. In a tizzy of regret, Adam stood. Who was this guy to give advice? This guy who'd confessed the limits of his worth minutes into an afternoon call with Adam the day before. *Should our meeting tomorrow suggest as much, Adam, I'm happy to refer you to medical professionals.*

Mental health is health, God knows, but the priest didn't have to start there, did he?

Through a door that Adam hadn't noticed, a fully costumed priest walked in, his hand extended out toward Adam's.

Fr. Michael, the priest said. *Heard you enter. I was on the phone. You've been standing all this time?*

Oh no, Father, Adam said.

Please come in, Fr. Michael said.

Adam entered the inner office and witnessed a wholly woeful setting in need of renewal or renovation. He saw no appreciable sign of updates, maybe since the second World War. The wood was dark, the drapes faded, the walls forlorn, and the carpet worn and bare. If the intent was to portray to potential donors a parish long impoverished, the decorator served the cause well.

Sit down, please, Fr. Michael said. *I'll just close the door.* Fr. Michael sat facing Adam, no desk or table staged between them, and recounted in precise detail their phone call the day before. *Do I have that right, Adam?*

You do, Father, Adam said, impressed by Fr. Michael's recall. *Thanks so much.*

Very good, then tell me more.

His conscience and confidence both in shambles, Adam recounted his youth in the church—the calm, the solace, the comfort that he felt nowhere else—then launched into a valiant confession. *I grew up close to the church, Father. Mass on Sunday, daily prayer, but I've fallen away in recent years. I haven't been to Mass ...*

Fr. Michael interrupted him. *No, no, Adam. What matters is your faith. You shouldn't feel you need to attend Mass to approach me. My position is that it's up to me to attract you to the church, not up to you to make your presence visible to me.*

Adam relaxed his inhibitions, surprised that in mere minutes, a priest had earned his trust. *A relief to hear that,* Adam said, reassured by an open mind he hadn't thought to expect. Adam continued. He was forthcoming, offering memories he long cherished—trips downtown, the waterwheel—and details he hadn't uttered aloud, not even to Carmen in their early days: His mother's arms around him tight in the wake of his father's fury. His father's full-on vengeful screaming for no good reason his mother could see, other than rumors—years of rumors—that Crosby-Kent would move away. His guilt, after his mother died, for wishing his father had died instead. The slap in the face the river was, exploited and abandoned. By Adam's count, the phone rang long and went to voice twice while he was talking.

The river's decline has a hold on you.

It does, Adam said.

And your mother does too.

Adam gripped the arms of his ladderback chair.

What was your mother's name, Adam?

Mary.

You think of her often?

I do, Adam said.

Why not embrace Mary's memory by exploring the river's plight? Elbows resting on his knees, Fr. Michael leaned forward. *Your unrest is tangled up in her death— and, maybe, the death of her memory in the river's decline.*

Adam sat motionless.

Do you think you could learn more, get involved, and help turn a dying river into an opportunity—both for the river's sake by getting involved and for your sake by honoring your mother's memory?

I've wanted to, Adam said, releasing his grip on the chair.

An involuntary act, the release was, but an act that Fr. Michael noticed. *Good,* Fr. Michael said. *Don't run from, run toward,* he said. *We can't resolve what we run away from.*

3.

Beyond the library's double doors, a voice at the entrance called to ask, *Need a password today, Mr. Monti?*

Startled, Adam said, *Oh, no,* turning his head to see who spoke. *Back to the stacks today,* he said, pointing up to the floor above, catching a glimpse of the woman who spoke, impressed she'd forgotten neither his name nor a detail of his visit.

Climbing the steps of the spiral staircase, he recalled her patterned Bohemian clothes; dark hair down to the middle of her back; a headband, wristbands, hanging earrings; a silhouette thin in a healthy way. She was anything and everything Carmen wasn't.

At the table he had used before, Adam read editions of *The Evening Call.*

Piece after piece, the arc of story that Adam built left him uneasy. Over the past few months or so, much was made of the river's decline and little about revival. On decline, a series of feature articles—posed in *The Call* as an exposé—reported troubling abuse and neglect. Toxic leaks at an ironworks plant that enjoyed a generous tax abatement, contaminated groundwater pooled in the brush beside a wire and cable mill, and wastewater pipes running to the river from a reckless auto parts plant. Several of the articles projected remediation costs into the millions of dollars. And one, a stunner to Adam's eye, summarized interviews with employees who reported bribes employers paid to silence complicit workers, including in one case overtime pay that doubled a waste-recovery manager's posted union salary.

On page one, above the fold, *The Call* reported that the statewide Press & News Guild awarded the team of byline authors an In-Depth Feature News Prize. By regional standards, quite a coup. But on plans for the river's future revival, *The Call* published one piece only. Notice of a scheduled City Council meeting disclosed a tentative agenda item to discuss a consultant's assessment of the river, a plan for water restoration, and the Council's proposal to seek restitution from each offending party. Another piece, days later, repeated the notice but scratched the agenda item. The message to Adam was clear. Benign neglect destroyed the river and few were engaged in the river's return.

With a pencil abandoned on the library table, Adam wrote in block letters, WHO IS THE RIVER WHO ISN'T, a phrase that had a comely rhythm but didn't make much sense to him. Staring at the page, pencil in hand, he inserted a comma after "the river," crossed out "is," replaced it with "was," then crossed out "the river" altogether, sat, and studied what he rewrote. WHO ~~IS~~ WAS ~~THE RIVER~~, WHO ISN'T. He couldn't quite say what he wanted to say—something, maybe, on now and then?—but he knew he was moved by the pieces he'd read. Is that what reading is all about?

Some moments later, his eyelids heavy, a headline reporting another toll aroused Adam's attention.

MILLRACE MONUMENT AT ODDS WITH FORCED REMOVAL OF INDIGENOUS POPULATION:

Totem Pole to be Removed

The piece reported that atop a mound at the Wilkinson millrace, a "ten-foot tall steel sculpture of Jedediah Wilkinson," the city's "first known European settler and successful early industrialist," would replace an "Indigenous-peoples Totem Pole" commemorating "sympathizers of Sekatau's

War"—a war that, in its wake, "removed Indigenous people by force."

Adam remembered the unkept pole—wooden, faded, graffitied, worn—an elaborately carved, neglected totem standing in an otherwise manicured setting that Wilkinson Weaving landscaped grandly. The Totem Pole wasn't new to Adam—it was there on visits in his childhood—but forced removal was new and unsettling. He came to the library on Fr. Michael's prompting—his mother's memory, a river in decline. Now, sitting where he was sitting, Indigenous people struck him more—or more than more, unexpectedly more.

Wouldn't removal of a people's totem to a way of life foregone have aroused his mother's outrage? Adam stood. He placed the chair under the table, left the room, and walked downstairs.

When was The Call first published? he asked.

1880s. 1885, I want to say.

Just wondering. Got sidetracked by a story on a monument and a Totem Pole I remember as a kid. Didn't know about Indigenous people—locally, their removal. That would have been before that, right? Before 1885?

Yes, she said, *and after too.* She explained that the land they were standing over was once the province of the Posquamicutt people; that Federal officials installed overseers to govern tribal reservations; and that the Posquamicutt tribe, though forcibly removed, survives in smaller numbers today.

Her recall of facts suggested to Adam more than a passing knowledge. *The Posquamicutt tribe, I'd heard of—back in school, I guess. They're relevant today?*

To me, they are. My grandfather served on the tribal council.

Oh, you're a Posquamicutt, then?

A descendant—my grandfather, Anna said.

You have an interest?

In the Tiler River, I do, he said. *But an article on forced removal took me by surprise. Grew up here and didn't know.*

They're actually the same issue, she said. *The river and the Posquamicutts.*

Ah, he said, stepping back. *The paper didn't say much more.*

There's books, several. But I can give you my take.

Sure, he said.

Glad to, she said, looking at her screen. *I'm free till three? Let's see, yes. A quick task now, then I'll come up where you are. Shouldn't be more than a few minutes.*

Seeing her name on a desktop nameplate, Adam said, *Okay, sure. It's Anna, right? See you soon. I'm Adam.* Walking toward the spiral staircase, Adam was encouraged she offered to talk and relieved she took the lead. Struck how quick the exchange progressed and aware of the many sides of Carmen, he didn't know—how could he know?—which part of Anna was the main one.

BACK AT THE TABLE, AWAITING ANNA, Adam glanced at a wall of paintings—a still life, portraits, a river landscape, and an oil that served as someone's take on New England's first Thanksgiving. What struck Adam in the often repeated daytime mural wasn't so much the abundant harvest on tables set for a sumptuous feast or the luminous sky—cloudless and bright, over a field of winter wheat—as it was the faces of Anglo-Europeans and Indigenous Americans, most in the throes of theatrical smiles on faces groomed meticulously, as if makeup artists had been engaged to complete the merry scene. A Native held in his outstretched hand the barrel end of a long-stem pipe, provoking Adam to sneak a smoke— maybe a drag in the men's room now, exhaling out an open window—but wouldn't that risk the scent of tobacco on his breath and clothes? He'd have to wait; he'd have to.

Hi, Anna said to Adam, walking toward his table.

Hi, he said, moisture forming on his upper lip. *Thanks for taking the time.*

No trouble. Let's get you up to speed.

Anna sat down across from Adam, placed a book in front of her, and in little more than several minutes offered a salient summary that would have required days of reading. A local controversy brewed when, as she told him, the town's appointed Tourism Council commissioned a sculpture of Jedediah Wilkinson for display on land that Wilkinson seized from Posquamicutts. Resisting a well-armed Anglo militia, the tribe was made to endure violence, theft, stockades, and forceable removal to barren land. The Totem Pole would be removed and replaced with a life size sculpture.

Sekatau's War was what? Adam asked.

The beginning of the end for Indigenous people, Anna said. *Sekatau's War—late sixteen hundreds—was their last stand against Anglo settlers. The chief Sachem—Sekatau—led the Posquamicutts in a bloody war over the takeover of tribal land. Hundreds of colonists were killed, slaughtered—and dozens of colonies destroyed. The War then turned the colonists' way— ammunition, medicines—and effectively came to a bitter end when Sekatau was caught by colonists, who resorted to torture and dismemberment. They shot, hung, and beheaded him. An asymmetric Treaty ended the war.*

Asymmetric?

They got more than we did, she said.

Your grandfather, a tribal elder?

A member of the tribal council, yes. One of a dozen or more— though, none with any appreciable power with the state—or influence, even. But oh boy, could he carry on in the oral tradition! Through him I learned to sympathize—then over the years it took on a life of its own for me. Atrocities on both sides. For me, though, it comes to this. There's plenty of Europeans all around here—you, for one—but far fewer tribal descendants anywhere near their land.

You said they're the same issue—the river, the Posquamicutts?

I did, they are, Anna said. *Had the Posquamicutts not been removed from their land, the culture and traditions on which the tribe survived would have protected the river's health.*

How so? he asked.

Anna leaned forward, elbows on the table, each of her hands in play. *Has it occurred to you—really, has it?—that in the middle of a jungle or dense forest, where animals tear each other apart—blood, bone, guts, hide—and defecate wherever they please, the forest presents like virgin land?*

Not till you said it, Adam said.

To the tribes, the idea's leave the land like the animals would, not like civilized settlers did.

Adam sat with his hands folded.

So here we are, centuries later, erecting a monument to a single settler who exploited the land and a pristine river that was left pristine by generations of Posquamicutts—that nothing more than a worn totem stands in place to commemorate.

Knowing he could offer nothing on point, Adam said something else. *You okay on time?* he asked, threatening his legitimate excuse to peer straight into light brown eyes that were somehow surrounded by whiter whites than he thought he'd seen in person before.

You're right! My gosh, Anna said.

Adam leaned back.

Hope this helped, she said to him. *Here, here's a book by Jim Harrison, prolific writer. Died in the twenty tens, I think. Dalva. His work's first rate. You got a card?*

A card?

Library card, she said.

Oh, no.

She slid the book to Adam's side of the table. *They'll get you one downstairs,* she said.

Thanks, Anna. This was great. And thanks for the book.

Part of the job, she said to him, beginning to stand.

Seated and looking down at the book, Adam asked, *You up for coffee later?*

She looked down, turned, walked toward the staircase, then looked back over her shoulder. *The Tourism Council meets Thursday night to air the Wilkinson sculpture. I'm speaking.* She didn't wait for Adam to answer.

Lighting a Lucky on the way back home, it occurred to Adam that empathy for displaced people was the only side of Anna he'd seen—an upgrade from Carmen, to say the least.

THE McDEVITT MUNICIPAL WELFARE BUILDING, renamed for an innovative retail baron but erected as the local welfare office, captured the city's imagination, partly for an ornamented Beaux Arts dome and mostly for an acutely-angled frontage, not unlike—though less pronounced than—Manhattan's iconic flatiron building. Strangely, a concrete-paneled window infills the entry under the dome, causing Adam no little confusion finding his way into the building, used now as the library's annex, though a couple of blocks away.

Reported in *The Call* as 7 p.m., the 6:45 p.m. meeting had since begun by the time Adam found the entrance, a flight of stairs, and one among the few empty seats in a room a fire marshal's placard read, CAPACITY 110.

Tiered and wider than it was deep, the room seemed far too raucous to Adam, at least for a serious business meeting—side talking, laughter, commotion in the seats and at the door. Adam had missed the opening comments, likely from the council, if anyone else. Now, minutes into the meeting, audience members spoke one by one, in line behind a microphone positioned in a center row. A hearing more than a meeting, he thought. Several spoke briefly on Wilkinson's achievements (courageous pioneer ... first settler ... the waterwheel), but none on the totem till Anna spoke. Is this what she meant by speaking tonight? Shoulders back, no notes in hand, wearing a pair of horn-rimmed glasses, she seemed to have the demeanor and stance of someone who commands respect.

Anna's remarks were replete with insights. *The Posquamicutts, a proud and resourceful people, were dominating far longer than they were dominated. Over thirty thousand years,* she said, a nod to the tribe's long reign. Quite apart from separatists, *The Posquamicutts fought bravely with union soldiers against warring tribes, often with no munitions in hand.* And most curious to Adam, *A people are a whole contraption,* she said, *some with mercy, some with flaws, leaving victims on both sides, not just one or the other one*—a concession to the baggage each side carries.

Later in her comments—was she talking too long?—Anna offered a telling remark that weighed on Adam in at least two ways. *Much like Elizabeth Hardwick wrote in the aftermath of Watts,* Anna said, *the Posquamicutts had 'fallen away from all but the most diminished hopes.'* For one thing, "diminished hopes"—so true, Adam thought, for many of us. And for another, someone employed in a library, you figure to be well read. But to have read so broadly—Hardwick, Harrison, who knows who else—was nothing less than a marvel to a man who hadn't read a book himself, not even the one she gave him.

Others spoke, a number of others. Mercifully, the meeting drew to a close. Someone might have said "adjourned" but Adam hadn't heard.

Anna walked from her seat toward Adam, looking elsewhere most of the way.

Courageous pioneer? Adam said to Anna, in a reaching attempt—a sarcastic attempt?—to signal to her his disapproval of the Council's side of the debate.

She smiled, spoke to a thankful supporter, then said, *Yes, to some.*

Coffee? he asked.

A drink, she said, walking toward the meeting room door, then out toward the stairs and the first floor entrance, not bothering to offer the body language that would show she knew he followed—a glance, maybe, was that too much? *This way,* she said on the crowded sidewalk, motioning with an index finger. Adam followed, entered a bar some steps behind her, and followed her to a high-top table near a swinging kitchen door.

Anna called to a passing waitress, *Sam Adams for me. You?* she asked, turning to Adam.

Bud, he said.

No Bud products, the waitress said. *Distributor's strike. Sam okay?*

He nodded and the waitress walked away.

What'd you think? Anna asked. *A cause worth fighting for?*

He nodded, shrugged, and tilted his head. *Tabled for now. Is that what they did?*

Right, there's more to come, she said.

What you said tonight, you said, 'there's victims on both sides.' I thought you'd take the Posquamicutt's side completely.

That word, 'completely.' Rare that one side's completely right or completely wrong. Not completely, despite what each side cherry picks to say.

But Native Americans were wronged, right?

Look, she said, *I'm trying to acknowledge both sides. Claude Levi-Strauss, a French anthropologist, documented the Nambik-wara, an Indigenous people on the Amazon River who successfully avoided the Europeans till the twentieth century. The <u>twentieth</u> century, they held off till! He wrote—I think this applies—that they were haunted by the Europeans because they knew that the Europeans were a people as fearful <u>and</u> as hostile as the Nambik-wara were themselves. There's menace coming from both sides—the Europeans, the Posquamicutts—but the ones who were already there on the land, they're easier to root for.*

A concession then, right? Adam said.

Not to appease them, not at all. Merely to speak the truth. I try to convey to the other side—don't know if I do, don't know if they're listening!—I'm willing to admit this isn't a zero-one, all-right-no-wrong. Now, that aside—that important concession—no one can argue the Posquamicutts weren't here first. The torment exacted on them was because they were here at all. In short, the other side wants a zero-one and all we want to do is share. We take where we are—the Totem Pole. And they take where we aren't!

The 'we,' though, is the tribe alone? Adam asked.

Yeah, well, weren't you listening?

What?

The intros.

Got there late, he said.

Each side did an opening statement. Five minutes each. The Council first—they went over—then us, the Posquamicutts.

You spoke for them?

No, the Tribal Council. A member, full-blooded Posquamicutt, representing the full bloods, the partials, and, as he said, pointing to the audience, 'our sympathizers'—that's the three prongs of the 'we.' They listen better to full bloods—and that's part of the problem. Great job, he did. Made clear our group, folks like me, is committed, growing, and active in the community—rallies, local candidates, even door to door.

Growing? he said.

Well, the numbers, a minor fib. They got more. Again tonight. Not long back, our numbers were even smaller. A few supporting the Posquamicutts—the sympathizers—then a few more. We need more.

Full blooded, that matters? he asked.

To the government, it has, in legislation through the twentieth century. Only full blooded, they said, thereby decreasing their take on our numbers.

Your take? he asked.

Not just mine, ours. Holding us to full blood denies the diversity in every other walk of life. What, every legislator is full blooded to wherever their ancestors came from?

<u>Dalva</u>'s a novel, I saw, right?

What?

The book you gave me.

Oh. You couldn't tell for yourself?! Anna asked, smiling in an all-too-telling way that returned his earlier sarcastic volley. *Not that you thought it a hybrid. You just couldn't tell?*

But don't I want nonfiction? he asked, figuring it's better to ask outright, than to ask her what a "hybrid" is.

Up to a point, sure you do. But beyond that, fiction goes to emotion in ways that pure facts don't. Look at it this way. If you're planning a trip to Columbia, say, then Garcia-Márquez, his fiction; Native Americans, then Harrison's fiction. You need a story to animate the facts.

Why Adam thought—and was close to saying—does so much out of Anna's mouth arrive like a classroom lecture? True, he wasn't close to saying, but still. *Got it,* he said. *I see that,* holding back what he couldn't say. *If I go to Columbia, I'll get a tour book.*

You're not married, she said.

Was, how'd you know?

You have time on your hands, she said. *Tell me, how did it start to end. Not end, not that. <u>Start</u> to end.*

Start to end?

Yeah, the first sign. What wasn't spoken?

Adam paused. *A look. An inward look, I guess. As if she's there and isn't there.*

Good answer, she said. *It's often that, except for the two-faced scoundrels. What was her name, if you don't mind my asking?*

Carmen.

Speaking terms?

No. Kept my last name, though—or <u>did</u>. Go figure.

Too much trouble, changing names. Head now angled to the side, she asked, *Tell me, why the quarter zips?*

What?

Quarter zips—like the other day, the time before, and the one you got on now.

He felt a blush of warmth on his face. *What about it?* he asked.

It's summer, she said, smiling broadly. *I better get going.*

Want to get a bite?

Adam, you're a nice guy, I can tell that. I'm recruiting you, you can't tell that?

What? he said.

You can't tell, can you?

He didn't answer.

You saw the split. We need people—sympathizers—people who have time, like I know you have nights, free to do as you please. And I'm guessing days too, from your visits to the library.

Well … he began, eyebrows raised.

Join us, Adam. We need a broader reach to prevail. More than just our own.

Tables full, the gathering crowd was standing mostly, some so close to their high-top table that the hem of a woman's short-waist blouse dangled over Adam's napkin. Anna reached for the one-round check (*Recruiting,* she said to Adam, smiling), stood to signal the evening's end, and walked out first like she'd walked in (*Stay warm,* she quipped, looking back at him). She disappeared in the dark of night, Adam walking well behind, little more than a willing pawn in the accidental chemistry of fate.

NORTH BEND WAS THE SORT OF MID-SIZE TOWN where a local wasn't likely to see what they couldn't see somewhere else. Take crime. In all the editions of *The Evening Call* Adam came across, police reports, published often, rarely amounted to all that much—car thefts, yes, more than enough; accidents, yes, though few reports of serious harm. Even the notice of Carmen's arrest. The crash and arrest took their toll, though she wasn't injured and it could have happened anywhere else. But the plight of the river, *that* was different—and it was because of an Indigenous tribe's disrupted way of life. Sure, this happened in other towns—anywhere Indigenous people were—but this is the town where Adam was born.

Sitting alone at his kitchen table, nursing a second or third beer, holding a disputed past-due bill, Adam's sense of introspection caught him by surprise. Surveying the streets of North Bend proper, you wouldn't expect, from what's around, to find a local resident loathe to read a book. Not with a handsome public library, erected on land the Posquamicutts roamed, near a river the tribe revered, and a well-appointed nearby bookstore adorned with a wholly cunning name—Acorn Books—that signaled the nurturing worth of books. Foot traffic near and around each building offers ample evidence that North Bend residents read books. Apparently, lots of books. Not just news and online gossip. Full length books. And this in a town wholly wanting in fortune, growth, or a four-year college.

Odd that this would occur to Adam—the beers that he'd been nursing maybe?—but there's no denying that, since visiting the library's hallowed halls, his failure to read had weighed on him. More than he would have thought it would. As much, he had to admit to himself, as realizing in later life that his father likely couldn't read.

Adam would have to read a book.

He would. *Dalva.* He'd read that. It was here somewhere, wherever he put it, and surely wasn't due back yet. He'd start in the morning—if he could. There was that business with the past-due bill.

In the morning, Adam rose early, brewed a pot of strong coffee, and pulled an upholstered rocking chair near the bay window. This was great. A book in hand, coffee in reach, and a cold, steady, pouring rain on the other side of the window. He could see what people saw in this—the hunkering down, the sense of wonder, the urge to be transported.

No few pages into the book, he fell asleep instead.

Startled by a truck or sudden thunder, the sense of wonder had abandoned him. He'd had enough, enough of that. No way, three hundred pages, no. A book the table of contents said included three books! And the very first page, a jumble. What book opens with, "It was today—rather yesterday, I think …"? Make up your mind. *Shouldn't I give the book a chance, only one sentence in?* Adam thought. Try as he might, he was powerless to continue. It wasn't in his nature to continue. He'd never read three hundred pages, not even when he had to—if even he'd have known he had to, his listening ear falling deaf on anything a teacher said.

He'd find the Wikipedia page. See what it said and go from there. He did from his phone in less than a minute but found that the page repeated what the jacket copy said. There was a summary and detailed guide at a site that seemed suspicious, but the page offered little more, then demanded a king's ransom to get to the heart of the book. Next best thing—*first* best thing?—he'd dump reading any of this and see if they made a movie. They did. With Farrah Fawcett as Dalva, they did. That's what he'd do, he'd watch the movie—and as a bonus, her. In her prime in another time, she wasn't a force when he came of age but enough of a force in entertainment lore that she'd be worth a look. He'd find the movie. He'd do that, no more than that.

No streaming that he could find online, though there was a dated DVD which, at a wholly outrageous price, would cost more than the book would. He wanted to learn, to understand—to come to grips with a grievous plight that continued to have an edge to it.

He'd think about it. About a reason to adopt the cause. There *was* what Fr. Michael said. There *was* what his mother would have said. There *was* the time he had in hand. And the means of support in what remained of the loot his father left behind.

Days later, the bill resolved, he drove to the public library.

Hey, Anna said to Adam. *More work on the Tiler River?* she said, smiling. *Or the Native American—was that it?*

Adam didn't need the sarcasm. He started it and wished he hadn't. *I'm here to work,* he said.

The library?

The cause, your cause—the Totem Pole.

The smile gone, she looked at him. *Really?*

Yes.

Mean to tell me the recruiting worked? She managed another smile.

That, yes. The pole, more. People are getting the shaft here.

Smile relaxed, brow furrowed, *No strings attached?* she said.

No strings, he said. *I've got the time.*

Time's not enough. Gotta believe in the cause, my friend. No ulterior motives here. Not for this, not here.

No motives, Anna. I'll help you. Nothing seemed more important to Adam than dismantling Anna's preoccupation with his ill-fated interest in her.

Fair enough, Anna said. *But tell me, why the interest?*

The interest?

Yeah, why the interest? she asked.

Adam paused, looked at the wall and then at her. *I never know what to say when you ask—because I wouldn't be saying if you hadn't asked.*

That's your answer? she said.

Well, visiting the river recently, after trips there as a kid. The change in the river. A Fr. Michael at Mother of God. Talked to him. Then, you know, the Totem Pole got under my skin.

You know him well, the priest? Rely on him?

Never met him before I called, made an appointment. Religious when I was a kid. Expected the worst, but he got to the point in minutes.

What can you do to help us? Anna asked.

What do you need?

We've got front lines; we've got back office.

Handled cash, accounted for cash. Accounting at a company out of town.

What company?

Coro, he said.

A neighbor worked there. A solderer, I think.

Right, a metal findings shop.

You're trained? she asked.

Yeah, sure. Coro trained me. A bookkeeping class in school, too.

That would be a ramp-up for us. Some pitch-in but mostly me. Collecting, deposits, bills. You'd do that?

Sure. It'd let me get my feet wet. Ease in through the paperwork.

It would, she said.

The tribe doesn't have an accountant? Like companies do, a CFO?

We don't. We should.

What's the cash for? Adam asked. *Wouldn't think you'd need much.*

You'd be surprised. For the monument initiative alone, there's ads, rentals—space, equipment, amplification at outdoor rallies. Then there's the tribe's other initiatives. An environmental protection program, a childcare fund, emergency management, warming centers.

How do you raise money, dues?

No, no dues. Solicitations—email, snail mail, grants from foundations, local companies.

Wilkinson? he said, smiling.

Fat chance, she said.

I can help. Could handle it, if you want.

You do spreadsheets?

Enough, he said.

You were in the service?

No, 4-F. Asthma that's not too bad—but bad enough for them, I guess.

Got a passport?

No, I got no passport. Never needed one.

Anna sat back in a swivel chair.

Why the questions? Adam asked.

Either would have done a background check.

Adam shifted his weight, foot to foot.

I'll think about it, Anna said. *Come to a meeting Thursday night?*

Sure, when and where?

She told him.

Rather than walk to his car directly, Adam descended the library steps, turned toward the river blocks away, and walked along deserted streets he hadn't walked in years. Steps from the entrance to Acorn Books, in sight of the door—the very handle—he opened as a kid, Adam stopped, turned his head to the empty street, and saw on the sidewalk a manhole cover he'd forgotten his mother had told him once is inscribed with the year that she was born. He walked to the cover—tarnished, aged, the lettering worn—and into the face of a steady breeze, his thinning hair sharing the fortune of a falling leaf—lifting, soaring, drifting, floating—thoroughly the wind's obedient creature on a path consigned to whim.

4.

Hundreds of years is too long to live by the rule of an oppressor. The Posquamicutts did—and do now, Adam came to learn.

No one's here, Adam said.

You're here, Anna said.

You said six.

For you, she said, smiling. *Sit back there and read—here.* She handed him sets of stapled pages clamped in a medium binder clip.

Pages in hand, Adam looked to assess how many. Not too many, but the last thing he wanted to do was read. Give them back, walk from this? He looked at Anna, who was looking at him. He'd put up with it.

In a facsimile of a 1524 letter, Giovanni da Verrazano, an Italian explorer in service to France, reported to King Francis on a sponsored overseas voyage west. Verrazano had landed on a "previously unknown foreign shore populated with many people," some of whom showed "great delight at seeing us." Communicating by gesture alone, the people showed "where we could most easily secure the boat and offered us some of their food." Disembarked, Verrazano witnessed "… many beautiful fields and plains full of great forests … palms, laurel, cypress, and other varieties of tree unknown in our Europe …" and "… other riches, like gold … an abundance of animals … lakes and pools of running water with various types of birds." Mindful of the King's lust for gold, Verrazano reported that, to his surprise "They do not value gold because of its color; they … rate blue and red above all other colors."

Here was a land abundant in riches and devoid of signs of civilization—no crowded streets, no horse drawn carriages, no nearby stench or sewage. This was the land of the Posquamicutts.

Looking back at the date of the letter, 1524, it occurred to Adam that Verrazano landed a century before the Pilgrims would and in the century after Columbus did. Scanning again the ancient letter, Adam lingered on two phrases—"delight at seeing us" and "do not value gold"—the first seemed an outsized stretch, the second ripe for exploiting.

Adam scanned the remaining documents to assess what he had left to read. Scholarly essays on exploration and on Sekatau's War, a broadside announcing the immediate sale of the Posquamicutt Reservation, an excerpted summary of the U.S. Indian Reorganization Act, a letter from First Lady Eleanor Roosevelt, and a document announcing the Posquamicutts as a federally recognized Indian nation. Adam was struck that some of the documents were photocopies of originals, likely uncolored by later day editorial slant. He'd read each document clear through, risking that Anna, a person of letters, might think he read too slow.

Reports of gold in Verrazano's letter brought other European voyagers and, thereafter, permanent settlers, who carried with them contagious disease that infected the immuno-compromised tribe. Domesticated livestock, brought from Europe, trampled the forest undergrowth and the fields Natives planted. More troubling, the settlers built imposing fences, forming permanent property lines, a sight offensive to a people averse to individual ownership.

Riches in reach, including gold, the land of the Posquamicutts would become the land of the Europeans.

A fierce leader when provoked, Sekatau, the Posquamicutt's chief Sachem, incensed by the settlers' land encroachment and by uninvited evangelism, staged a revolt in 1675. A bloody two-year conflict, Sekatau's War ended badly for the Posquamicutts. Sekatau dead, the survivors were forced to sign a treaty, the final step in detribalization. European sentiment firmly against them, the Posquamicutts were banished from their 3,200 acre ancestral land to ten acres of dense woods, rock, and uncleared hills miles from the nearest fresh water lake, farther from rich ocean fishing, and farther still from fertile soil to plant and harvest, spring and fall.

Adam was aware of relocation, but not to a land of meager size and feeble resources. A way of life interrupted, walls closing in.

In 1882, a century removed from Wilkinson erecting a weaving mill, the government published public notice that the legacy Posquamicutt Indian Reservation was available for private purchase. Sold in days, the Posquamicutts received no compensation, the proceeds directed partly to the state and partly to the U.S. Department of Interior, overseers of the Bureau of Indian Affairs.

Not until the 1934 Indian Reorganization Act—called by some Franklin Delano Roosevelt's "Indian New Deal"—did the U.S. government grant Indigenous people the right to preserve tribal land in a federal trust exempt from taxes, and to self-govern—although not to vote, a right denied Native Americans until the first federal civil rights litigation in 1957. Touched by a letter from Princess Yellow Wing, historian of the Posquamicutt tribe, Eleanor Roosevelt wrote from the White House in 1935:

Washington, D.C.

My dear Princess Yellow Wing:
I was very much interested in your letter and what you are trying to do for the Posquamicutt Tribe of Indians. I send you my best wishes for success.

Very truly yours, Eleanor Roosevelt.

The tribe was consumed in red tape and protracted litigation, and the government ignored the tribe in the decades following the 1930s, relenting in April 1983, a half century later, when the U.S. Bureau of Indian Affairs recognized the Posquamicutts as an independent nation in a government-to-government relationship, each one—the U.S. and the Posquamicutts—a sovereign nation. The Posquamicutts now had unilateral authority to regulate activity on tribal land and to preserve ancestral culture, just like other tribal nations, thereby completing the circle back to where—or, as Anna would say, *Well short of where*—the Posquamicutt nation had been before the settlers arrived. Centuries removed from a millennium of freedom, the Posquamicutts fought and finally won federal tribal status.

Gnawing now, Adam knew, was a revered but long neglected totem that, once removed, would erase from the town's public view a reminder of a forcibly displaced people and enshrine in its place a revisionist homage to a secular savior, who numbered among the tribe's oppressors. It would be as if—entirely as if—history began with Wilkinson's arrival. To the Posquamicutts, their memories long, that's when history ended.

Adam was moved. He hadn't known the gravity of the plight a tribal nation suffered on the ground he walks on now. Is this how an awakening begins—an awakening in oneself begins—as a poverty of communion suddenly exposed?

Rising from a desk at the head of the room, a stack of manila envelopes near, Anna watched Adam gather the stapled pages. *That's our story*, she said to him, turning to answer a knock at the door. *And all we want is a Totem Pole to remain on the grounds the tribe once lived. Too much to ask?* she said.

PLEASE COME IN, Anna said.

By Adam's count, three dozen people entered the room. A few may have been high school age but most were adults, skewed to the end of middle age. They moved toward parallel rows of tables, milling about and taking seats as if they'd done this often before. One, a man—maybe seventy-five?—caught Adam's eye. The red band of a Lucky Strike pack was apparent in the pocket of the man's plaid shirt, just like Adam's father's shirt. Smartly attired in well pressed clothes, a Pork Pie hat in hand, the man walked with an exaggerated stoop, his head tilted up and back, shuffling forward step by step, one leg doing most of the work, the other dragging behind. Might this have been Adam's father if he'd lived to that age? On entry, some people turned toward the man, greeted him, smiled at him, quipped with him—and he quipped back—but no one helped him in any way, other than standing aside. Adam was impressed, interpreting the scene as warmth from the man and respect from the others for his independence. The man smiled and responded warmly, someone who—unlike his father—Adam could take a liking to.

Moving to the front of the meeting room, Anna introduced Adam. *Folks, third row is Adam Monti. Raise your hand, Adam? Please welcome him.*

The group applauded.

Adam's taken an interest in our cause and, equally important—especially to me!—he's volunteered to take over our far too feeble bookkeeping role. Adam has the right background—accounting at a for-profit firm that should translate easily to a not-for-profit. The plan is for Adam to take over the day-to-day. Thanks, Adam!

Rather than tell Adam face to face—isn't that how hiring's done, even for a volunteer?—Anna announced his new role in front of the group at large. Had Anna somehow checked on him or simply trusted her gut? Either way, Adam sat peacefully, aglow in the opportunity release from a sordid past brings.

The meeting proceeded with Anna recounting the Council's stance—*Not a one has budged an inch*—facilitating questions, and explaining the need for volunteers, both to signal mounting interest and to work behind the scenes, like Adam. One of the questions and Anna's reply seemed to Adam instructive.

Anna, it's gratifying that we've had a stable turnout at rallies, including the Council meeting—but our numbers aren't growing.

Agreed, Anna said, *but here's another way to think of it. I think we can get away with one person alone—if it's the right person—to make an impression on the Council. Now, on that one, we'd want an influential voice, I think from the donor class. We need to focus on that. On someone from the high-end donor class the Council would respect.*

Anyone in mind? someone asked.

Maybe. Tom Simeone. Anyone know him, heard of him? No one answered. *He grew up here, through high school. A line of Posquamicutts from his grandparents back. Not full blood, but we've got to get away from that. Went to NYU, worked at Morgan Stanley in New York, investment banking. Runs a venture-capital firm now. Searching, I stumbled on an oil & gas holding company—Houston, I think—where he's on the board. As of last year, his holdings were north of 400 million dollars. That one holding alone. I don't know if he gets back here or identifies with us.*

Oh yes, a man in the back said—an older voice, maybe the man who impressed Adam. *Knew my daughter. Ran in the same crowd off and on—high school—but drifted away when he graduated.* Adam delayed turning around, missing his chance to see who spoke.

You know him? Anna asked.

Vaguely, as a kid, the man said, *when you said NYU—unusual for around here. I'd see him at the house.*

How much time do we have, Anna? someone else asked. *The Council's seeking proposals, drawings.*

Right, Anna said. *We'll need to move.*

We'll approach him? someone asked.

I'll approach him, Anna said. *The first obstacle's getting through to him. I'm working channels—happy to hear ideas—but I'll resort to a cold call if I have to.*

The meeting trailed off in interest to Adam—things about newsletters, ads, and catering that failed to hold his attention.

Watch your email, Anna said, adjourning the meeting.

Adam turned toward the man who impressed him, but a group had gathered around the man, leaving little room to maneuver without trampling over them or interrupting him. Adam walked near and past Anna, who was speaking to a woman and a man.

Hold on, Anna said to Adam, then offered goodbyes to the woman and the man, and a louder goodbye to the those remaining. *Got a minute?* she asked Adam.

Sure, he said.

I brought these—what you'll need. Everything's in this bag, the records. And this—a signature authorization—to sign at the bank in person. I told them you'd be coming. You'll be the second signatory, just you and me. Checks require only one. Appear and sign in front of them. She placed the bag where Adam could reach. *There'll be bills to pay, end of the month, and the ones in here now.*

I should pay the bills? Adam asked.

Right, Anna said. *Soon as you sign the authorization.*

Will do, tomorrow.

Good, she said. *Anything else?*

I was thinking. What I read before—Sekatau's War. Driven by land encroachment it said. And by evangelism, Christian evangelism. I get the land encroachment part, but evangelism was just as important?

It was, Anna said, *partly for an obvious reason—don't push your beliefs on us—but more than that, Posquamicutts don't believe humans are any more important than any other living thing.*

Didn't think about that, Adam said.

They see it like this. With millions of species and billions of beings roaming the earth, it's absurd to presume that a God created all this solely and only—they'd have you believe—for humans to win a place in Heaven. We take ourselves too seriously. It's not about us. It's about everything there is.

Adam reached for the bag before him.

Think about it, Anna said. *Then think about how self-absorption flies in the face of how Posquamicutts think.*

Adam did think. Walking out to his parked car, he thought about what Anna said—particularly self-absorption—and also how petty his take had been on Carmen. Reach out to her, speak to her? Or would that be petty *and* self-serving? More important—now, at least—was the files Anna had given him. Anxious to take a look at the files, Adam made a beeline home. He was nervous—and shouldn't he be? He'd promised to assume some tedious chores, now what to do if he can't deliver?

He opened the bag on his kitchen table and began to dig in.

Compared to what he'd seen at Coro, the records appeared primitive. In fact, much like his own at home. A black faux-leather manual checkbook, prenumbered checks, a check register, deposit slips, month after month of two- or three-page bank statements, and a series of monthly cash flow statements simple enough for a child to prepare. Oh, the numbers were larger than his at home but nothing a bare-bones calculator app couldn't handle on his phone.

Probing further, he saw that Anna wrote a dozen or so checks each month—a thousand dollars here, a few thousand there, several others in the hundreds. And a smaller number of bank deposits, larger in total than the checks going out. Two deposits caught his eye, ranging from five to ten thousand dollars a month, one from the U.S. Bureau of Indian Affairs and another from the Department of Indian Health Services. Anna had mentioned spreadsheets to him but hadn't mentioned using them—and likely wouldn't. There didn't seem to be a need, not from what Adam could see.

Should be easy, Adam said to himself. *A piece of cake,* he said out loud.

ADAM DIDN'T MIND PAYING BILLS, reconciling bank accounts, or keeping bank and other records in some semblance of order. Nor, for that matter, would he mind presenting financial reports at meetings. He planned to invoke the monotonous rote he'd heard from Coro's accountants often. Like "receipts exceed expenses by this; balance end-of-the-month is that." Keep it simple, keep it brief, keep them out of the weeds. The work, fine, he was fine with that—though reports would be a bore to him, and no doubt everyone else. He'd complete the work, give his report, and answer questions if some came up—like one at his next tribal meeting, delayed for several months.

Adam, may I ask that going forward you compile a list of what the checks are for?

Sure, Anna. I can do that.

Not who-to in detail, Anna said. *Categories of what-for. Rentals, mailings, things like that.*

Could you do that now? someone asked, looking at Adam.

How 'bout year-to-date next time? Anna said. *A fuller accounting than Adam's ready for now.*

Glad to do that, Adam said, staring the questioner down. Somehow, he felt threatened. Then he saw what he didn't expect. The man who had impressed him so—the man he saw at the last meeting—was slouched in his seat, sleeping.

The boredom of his reports aside, it was fair to say that Adam had his eye on the ball and that he was building trust. Anna embraced his full engagement in the dense details that finance the cause—as much, he thought, as she would have embraced him if he were active in the cause more, the role that many of the others play. Although not an elder, she was the force behind the resistance and, more to the point, relished leaving the details to him. And the details demanded Adam's attention, almost every day.

About to bring the meeting to a close, someone asked, *The guy in New York, any luck?*

Couldn't reach him directly, Anna said, *but I spoke by phone with an assistant, who said Simeone himself no longer supports non-profits individually—only through his foundation, which accepts applications and does the vetting. I gave him a sense of what we're about. I think it's a matter of trust.*

Should have sent your grandfather! someone quipped.

Like he was one who couldn't be trusted! Anna said, bringing the meeting to a close.

A woman offered a knowing reaction, *Kit was the very essence of trust,* suggesting to Adam that Anna's grandfather had been well known and liked. Leaving his seat, Adam approached Anna. He wanted to invite her out for a drink but thought the better of reigniting suspicions about his interest in her.

Your grandfather, Adam said. *Still active in the tribe?*

Not anymore, Anna said.

What's his name?

Kit Noka. Kit's short for 'Kitchi'—means 'courage' in Ojibwe.

A different tribe? Adam asked.

One of the more populous tribes in North America—from the Midwest mostly, the Great Lakes.

He's Posquamicutt, though, right?

Yeah, his parents—my great grandparents—both Posquamicutts, traveled to Michigan. Liked 'Kitchi'—the meaning—then got to calling him 'Kit' later. Well into old age now.

Tribal council, right? Adam asked.

Right, he was. Middle of the fight in the eighties—federal status.

Your parents? Adam asked. *Involved too?*

Anna paused. *Never met my father. Posquamicutt, my mother said. She died when I was a kid. Know more about her from my grandfather, her father, than from memory.*

Your grandmother. She alive?

Died with my mother. Anna said. *Accident. Car accident. Drunk driver, my grandfather said—but I'm not sure which car had the drunk driver. Never asked, just heard things here and there. 'Liquor had its way with them,' I overheard him say.*

Does he come around?

Afraid not, dementia. Knows me—or did last visit. In memory care.

Does he know about the monument?

Last thing he did know. She pulled her bag over her shoulder. *Gotta run. Visiting him.* Walking out, she said to Adam, *He knows I'll be there. Trusts me on that,* she said smiling. *Nights he remembers, he does.*

Trust apparently mattered to Anna. The word kept coming up. And trust mattered to what Adam was thinking—and thinking again as he left the meeting. Adam was thinking— he'd said to himself, walking out—*Anna has bank statements mailed to me and I sign and mail checks myself—that's trust.* He stopped, stood in place for a moment, then walked to his car and drove home.

GUIDED BY PRINCESS YELLOW WING and an area anthro- pologist, the Posquamicutts in 1958 opened a museum to curate the tribe's artifacts and to maintain a cultural emersion center, open to the public. The museum sits on tribal land the Posquamicutts had been banished to. On Anna's suggestion, Adam arranged a visit. *To get a sense for the culture,* she said, *apart from what was done to them.*

Driving along in fair weather, Adam's mind wandered. Why didn't Carmen confront him sooner with the fraud that he committed? Why didn't Adam plead with her for a chance at full redemption? What else between them went unsaid? Maybe for her, the emotional freedom to abandon who she wasn't—and did. Maybe for him, an oddly peace- ful emotional umbrella hovering over a brief connection to someone entirely willing—at first. He parked his car, entered the museum, and changed the subject in his mind, like anyone does when answers seem protracted. The subject now was a fading culture, reduced to a museum.

Once a Native American restaurant serving tribal rec- ipes, the museum holds over 15,000 artifacts. Donated by Posquamicutts, the artifacts include documents, gear, cere- monial costumes, Sekatau's headdress, and a vast assortment of mounted mammals—beaver, otter, and one brown bear, among them. Adam touched the bear's coarse fur and a four-inch long canine tooth, but was struck more by an adjacent display titled, "The Rhetoric of Erasure"—a tangible summary of a tribe ignored or otherwise forgotten. The U.S.

history Adam learned began with the European's arrival, over-looking that the Posquamicutts, once the dominant people on the land, prospered long before—and prospers today in smaller numbers, immersed fully in modern culture while observant of ancient tribal customs. The realization of ignoring and forgetting had been creeping up on Adam—the rhetoric, the language that erased a thriving nation. Not only had settlers replaced the tribe but erased their culture after.

Hello, welcome, a voice said.

Adam turned. *Hello.*

Can I help you, direct you? the woman said. Older, maybe seventies, she was wearing wholly contemporary clothes, not the contemporaneous Native costume Adam had expected. Nevertheless, her clothes reminded him of the style Anna typically wore. Her earrings, for instance—hanging, dangling, turquoise stones that seemed to evoke the museum's culture.

This display—erasure, Adam said. *How did—how <u>does</u>—that happen?*

Yes, well, the most powerful tool in erasure is silence. Silence alone withholds reminders. Lacking reminders, people forget.

Hadn't thought of it that way, Adam said. *Thought about what was done. Not what wasn't done or said.*

Exactly, she said. *Leads to false understanding—at a minimum.*

Interesting. How so? Adam said, then realized that, unintentionally, his question may have amounted to a challenge.

Well …

Adam interrupted. *Just trying to put a finger on it,* Adam said.

Of course, sure. Here's an example. A visitor said to me, 'You're wearing turquoise'—I was, these earrings—'but don't you know that's the color of the Southwest Indians, not the Posquamicutts? Get your history straight,' he said.

Confrontational. What did you say? Adam asked.

His was a statement, not a question. I smiled. He wasn't looking for an explanation.

He was wrong? Adam asked, treading again on the threshold of challenge.

He was, she said. *Native Americans have a long history of trading artifacts between tribes—and wearing the artifacts traded. A sign of friendship. A conference in Phoenix, I traded a pair of traditional Posquamicutt earrings with a Navajo. This pair I'm wearing now.*

Interesting.

The trouble is, because of erasure, our culture isn't understood. You're interested in the Posquamicutts?

Yes, grew up in North Bend. I volunteer up there—the Totem Pole—just bookkeeping for now—the Wilkinson ...

... A tragedy, tearing the pole down. Thanks for volunteering. My cousin does too—retired IRS—walks with a limp?

The older man at the meetings? Adam thought. *Not sure I know him,* Adam said and then thought, *IRS? Too accomplished to keep the tribe's books?*

How'd you get interested?

I happened upon it in the newspaper—at the library—and met a librarian ...

Anna.

Right. I had the time and she—they—had a need for some bookkeeping. Backoffice.

It's a good cause.

Is, she said. Her cell rang. *So nice to talk,* she said turning. *Do look around.*

I will, Adam said and did, lingering at several displays. The Posquamicutt tribe's traditional seal—tomahawk, star, the rising sun—that Princess Yellow Wing carved in 1934 and a display of Edison "Tarzan" White, a Posquamicutt athlete, who competed in the 1936 Olympic marathon, held in Nazi Germany. Walking toward a wall of photos, Adam was attracted to a set of grainy photos, one a close up—a portrait, posed—of an Indigenous boy. Expressionless, the boy's chest and shoulders were draped in woven animal skin, his head obscured by a child-size headdress, feathers and all, sparking for Adam a memory of a Christmas morning when Santa left a Native headdress Adam took as a child's version of a chief's crown—not realizing, not until now, that children wore them too.

Engrossed by the image—the headdress, mostly—Adam failed at first to realize that his phone was buzzing in his pocket. He sneaked a peak, saw FR. MICHAEL, hurried out, and returned the call. Fr. Michael answered on the first ring.

Tell you why I called, Adam. I thought we'd get together.

Sure, meet for coffee? Adam said.

Could but how 'bout my office, here. Friday okay?

Sure, I can do that, Adam said.

I was thinking the afternoon, three. That work?

I'll make it work.

No trouble? Fr. Michael asked.

No, no. I'll see you then.

See you then, Adam.

Standing beside his car door, Adam lit a Kool from a flip-top pack, inhaled deep like his father would, and exhaled long—as long as his lungs had air to give—till the gasp for new breath brought the relief that only fresh clean air could bring. Eyes shut tight, the soothing warmth of sun on his face, Adam barely moved, other than raising a hand to his lips and breathing deep and long.

NOW MORE THAN EVER, IF EVER BEFORE, Adam seemed to understand the poverty of his expectations. Bliss at first, then a rift between him and a younger Carmen that drove a broken marriage. Respect at first, then a gulf between him and an aging father that drove misguided contempt. Immature, is that what he was—and is still now? The immaturity that startles us wandering onto a playing field another player on the field commands. Or if not, then maybe what it is, is chance reminders of a misled youth who lacked imagination.

Driving alone in pouring rain, he thought what he'd been thinking about was insight into missteps—and a youth's missteps, at that. Adam felt good about himself. And why shouldn't he? He was on his way to see Fr. Michael to relate how well-timed sober advice had directed Adam to support a cause that would have made his mother proud. He was coming to grips with memories of a wife and a deceased father, the two main tensions in his life, and coming to value a priest and a deceased mother, the two main influences on his life. *All's good,* he'd heard people say in the wake of a worry they'd overstated. The rain was heavy, the thunder loud, but it might as well have been rays of sun shining overhead.

Adam parked, opened the door, and walked to the church entrance. There was spring in his step that he would have exploited, save for the puddles, wide and deep. He climbed the slippery steps slowly, retracted an oversized golf umbrella, then walked past pews in the empty church and opened the Sacristy door. Fr. Michael, sitting alone, rose at once to greet him.

Adam, yes, right on time.

Adam walked in.

Here, put your coat and umbrella there, Fr. Michael said pointing.

Adam smiled, relaxing in Fr. Michael's warmth—his command of the room, his presence. *Great to see you, Father,* Adam said, reaching to shake Fr. Michael's hand. *I have so much to tell you.*

Here, in here, Fr. Michael said, pointing toward, *my inner office*—the same office, Adam knew, where Fr. Michael changed his life.

Walking ahead, Fr. Michael opened the door, stood aside, and watched Adam walk in.

Adam stopped at once.

He faced two people, seated.

Anna was in a wingback chair and Carmen in the ladderback where Adam had sat himself. Stoic, silent, posture erect, Anna and Carmen stared at him.

I know what you've been up to, Anna said, a manila folder on the table beside her. Carmen's arms were folded below her chest, as if to impose a wall between them wider than the wall she'd imposed before.

One hand fiddling keys in his pocket, the other gripping his leather belt, Adam looked at neither of them.

Adam, listen, Fr. Michael said. *Anna approached me by phone and, on her behalf, I reached out to Carmen. Anna recalled both our names, sought us out, and, in a conference call Anna initiated, she raised troubling allegations. I proposed an intervention, a first step to hear you out—if you're willing.*

Looking at the floor, looking like a child who'd spilt his milk, Adam focused on "intervention," the urgency of the word.

Sit here, over here, Fr. Michael said, pointing to a couch. *I'll sit there, beside you.*

Anna stared directly at Adam, one hand resting on the folder. Carmen was watching Fr. Michael, her arms folded tight.

You know what this is about? Fr. Michael asked. Carmen looked at Adam. Adam didn't answer.

You wish not to speak, Adam? It's your right, Fr. Michael said. *I won't ask you to say more than you want to say.*

Well, I'll speak, Carmen said. *Not your first rodeo.*

Adam felt his heartbeat quicken, felt the cold in his feet and hands. He said nothing.

I have records, Anna said. *All of it reviewed and confirmed by a member with experience.*

Adam was speechless, literally speechless, his vocal cords unable to gather the timbre to utter an audible sound. He swallowed once, then swallowed again. His throat was parched, seeming to Adam about to close. His nerves had triggered a physical reaction, unlike any he'd felt before.

Won't you sit? Fr. Michael said.

Federal funds, Anna said.

Adam felt sweat build on his brow, in his hair, on his hands, his armpits. His tongue was immobile, swollen with fear, the beats of his heart rapid and deep. Worse, the arrival of nausea, chills. Never before having felt this before, he thought he was—was sure he was—on the verge of panic, if not worse, if this is what the verge of panic is. He didn't speak, hadn't sat. He tried to inhale deep but couldn't. He knew, he was sure, that time would pass—the days, the weeks, the months would pass—but not this moment now, not this.

Acknowledgments

I am grateful to editors of publications where stories in this book first appeared, some in different form:

"Indifferent Limbs," *The Massachusetts Review* (excerpts appear as linked verse in *Uncertain in the Worst Way*)

"Nights," *New Limestone Review*

"Beached on White Sheets," *North Atlantic Review*

"Isn't It Better That She Knows?," *NOON*

"How Much I Must Have Looked Like Her to Her," *First Intensity*

"Their Version," *First Intensity*

"The Card Catalog," *The Heartland Review*

"Angst," *Avalon Literary Review*

"The Body Double of Making Do," *Interim*

"An Absence of Speech," *Tampa Review*

"Standing Perfectly Still on the Table," *Exacting Clam*

"Carp," *Red Rock Review*

"What Scrimshaw Leaves Unsaid," *Red Rock Review*

"A Daughter's Conviction," *The Louisville Review*

"Inside the Jewelry Store Window," *The Quarterly*

No measure of thank you equals the care the staff of Cornerstone Press displayed, an object lesson on craft and commitment. No one did more to shape the aesthetic and design of the book than Dr. Ross Tangedal, Director & Publisher, or to navigate alertly through editorial detail than Ellie Atkinson, Editorial Director. And no one's done more to influence me, or is more deserving of notice from me, than those who gather nearest to me. Jean, who knows— has always known—that love wants most for signs of love. Marc and Kristin, who've come so fully into their own but remind us still how a child takes purchase on the human heart. Michaela and Chad, who enable our entry into life for a third time. And Grace, Mia, Eva, Lea, Charlotte, and Louie, the young hearts to whom I dedicate this book—and in whose stories we're all invested.

David Ricchiute is the author of two poetry collections, *Uncertain in the Worst Way* (2020) and *So Everyone Else Will Know* (2018). His writing has appeared in *NOON*, *The Massachusetts Review*, *The Louisville Review*, and *Tampa Review*, among others. Born in Rhode Island, he lives in Granger, Indiana, and Villa Hills, Kentucky.